ALLIE FINKLE'S RULES FOR GIRLS

BEST FRIENDS AND DRAMA QUEENS

MEG CABOT

MACMILLAN CHILDREN'S BOOKS

First published 2009 by Macmillan Children's Books

This edition published 2010 by Macmillan Children's Books
a division of Macmillan Publishers Limited
20 New Wharf Road, London N1 9RR
Basingstoke and Oxford
Associated companies throughout the world
www.panmacmillan.com

ISBN 978-0-330-45381-3

1 3 5 7 9 8 6 4 2

A CIP catalogue record for this book is available from
the British Library.

Typeset by Intype Libra Ltd
Printed and bound in the UK by CPI Mackays, Chatham ME5 8TD

For Best Friends Everywhere

Special thanks to Beth Ader, Jennifer Brown,
Barb Cabot, Laura Langlie, Abigail McAden
and especially Benjamin Egnatz

Rule #1

It's the Thought That Counts

The best part about the holidays is showing all the cool stuff you got for Christmas to your friends.

This is a rule.

But when your friends all leave for Winter Vacation to go visit the beaches in Hawaii or their grandparents or their mom in Maine or whatever, it's really hard to show them that your grandma got your family the new PlayStation with Dance Party America, which you have played so many times (by yourself) that you are already up to level eleven.

It's especially hard when your parents and your brothers and your uncle are quite tired of playing Dance Party America and of hearing about it too. They wish that your friends would come home from Winter Vacation to play it with you almost as much as you do.

1

I did have one friend who was home from Winter Vacation: Sophie. But she broke her toe when we when we were playing Olympic figure skater on her hardwood floor in our socks. So she couldn't do Dance Party America with me. Plus she was kind of crabby about her sore toe and not having seen her true love, Prince Peter, in so long.

So by the time Winter Vacation was over I was so excited for school to be starting again to see everyone, such as Erica and Caroline, and also my friend Rosemary, whose family had gone to Hawaii for the break, that I could barely fall asleep the night before. Even Mewsie's gentle purring on the pillow beside my head couldn't make me doze off, and usually that does the trick. I had called Erica three times before bed, knowing her plane had gotten in, even though Erica lives right next door and Mom kept telling me to leave the Harringtons alone and let them Settle In From Their Vacation.

But Erica told me she'd seen Caroline at the baggage carousel at the airport, and that she had some big news, but that Caroline's dad had dragged her away before she could tell Erica what it was.

Big news! What could it be?

I hoped it wasn't anything bad. What if Caroline was moving permanently to Maine, where her mom

2

lived? This would be terrible! Pine Heights Elementary would be losing its champion speller!

I was really surprised when I woke up on Monday morning. Surprised that I ever fell asleep at all, I mean, because I was so excited to get to school and find out Caroline's big news.

As usual when I woke up though, Mewsie was massaging my hair. This is a morning ritual he performs daily. No one is quite sure why, and though I'd consulted all my cat-care books, there'd been nothing in them about kittens kneading their owner's hair every morning. Mewsie takes his hair kneading very seriously, and if I try to get up before he's done, he cries. But sometimes his tiny claws sink into my scalp and it really hurts. Also, his hair combing can make me late.

'Ow ow ow ow ow,' I said to Mewsie.

'Mew?' he said sleepily back to me. Seriously, he is the cutest kitten in the whole wide world. But he is also the weirdest. The hair combing is the least of it. When I try to make the bed, he gets mad, and jumps around with his back arched, making hissing noises.

I said he was weird. Although if you think about it in this way he fits perfectly into my family.

I untangled my hair from Mewsie's claws and

hurried to get my face washed and my teeth brushed and undo the mess Mewsie had made of my hair. I am not the kind of person who cares a whole lot about how she looks.

I mean, I care, in that I do not want to smell or go to school with sleep in my eyes like Joey Fields.

But at the same time, I am not going to wear blue eyeshadow to school like Leanne Perkins does, even though she is only in the fifth grade. Because that would just be insane.

Still, I tried to Make An Effort since it was the first day of the new semester. I put on all the new hair-clips that my brother Mark had gotten me, and some of the cherry ChapStick Kevin gave me, and I even wore my new wrap-around ballet sweater (even though I didn't have ballet lessons until Saturday and I was wearing jeans with my snow boots since it was snowing, so it didn't exactly match). I also packed up my new fringed suede tote bag with some of the Boxcar Children books I got, which happens to be a very old-timey series I started reading because my teacher, Mrs Hunter, keeps her old copies from when she was a girl in our classroom. But I can never read them in order, because someone else in our class keeps taking them out and reading them. Only I don't know who it is, so I can't ask her to please return them so I can read them too.

Now I won't have that problem, because I have my own.

Then, after a nutritious breakfast of hot oatmeal with raisins and brown sugar that Dad made for us kids, because Dad is in charge of breakfast, I rushed outside to meet Erica when she knocked on the front door.

'Let's go find out Caroline's Big News,' I yelled as I hugged her hello.

'How are you?' Erica yelled back. 'I missed you so much! Did you have a good vacation? Oooooh, I like your new bag. We had the best time at my grandma's house, I saw a dolphin—'

'That's great,' I said. 'Let's go find out Caroline's Big News!'

I grabbed Erica by the front of her puffa jacket and pulled her from the porch and towards the street so we could hurry up and meet Caroline and Sophie by the stop sign, from where we always walked to school together.

'Hold on,' Erica said. 'Shouldn't we wait for your little brother?'

'Wait for me,' yelled Kevin, who is only in kinder-garten and has to be walked by us to and from school every day because he's too young to walk by himself. He was still being put into his snowsuit by Mom.

'He'll catch up,' I said.

I couldn't understand why Erica wasn't as excited as I was to find out what Caroline's Big News was. It could be anything. It could be that she had found out her family had won the lottery and that they were moving to a castle in Switzerland.

It could be that it turned out she was adopted and her real parents were famous movie stars and that she was going to be starring in her own reality television show about what it was like to be adopted and then find out that your real parents were movie stars.

It could be that she'd gotten a horse for Christmas.

It could be *anything*.

'*Come on!*' I said.

It was kind of hard to run on the icy sidewalk all the way to the stop sign, but I managed to do it somehow, dragging Erica behind me and having to listen to Kevin yell, 'Hey, wait! Allie, wait for me!' the whole way.

And of course when we got to the stop sign we had to wait because I'd forgotten about Sophie's broken toe and that Caroline and Sophie always walked the whole way to school together and of course that meant Caroline would be walking slow because

Sophie could only walk slow and Caroline would be polite and wait for her to catch up.

So we had to wait for them for what seemed like a really long time with our toes and noses freezing. Kevin finally caught up with us, and Mark had had to walk him, so Mark was mad because that meant he couldn't ride his new BMX dirt bike to school on the first day back, in order to show it off to all his friends. He'd had to walk with it.

Apparently I was supposed to feel sorry for him about this, even though it was the only day in like a million days where Mark had had to walk Kevin to school, instead of me.

But even so, when he got to the stop sign, where Erica and I were waiting, Mark went straight up to me and punched me in the arm.

It didn't hurt, because I was wearing my winter coat, my ballet sweater, a turtleneck, a T-shirt, and an undershirt under that.

But of course I had to punch him back, only harder. Because I'm older, and I had to teach him that violence is never the answer.

This made Erica yell, 'You guys! Stop it! Can't we all just get along?' because she's a peacemaker and is always trying to make everyone in her own family, like her big sister, Missy, and big brother, John, stop fighting (not that this ever works).

It didn't work in my family either. My hitting Mark back made him drop his bike in the snow and then it got wet and so he started crying, because he was so mad.

And of course right then some of his friends rode by and saw him crying, which just made him even angrier.

So then he yanked his bike out of the snow and rode away with his face all red and teary.

This made me feel a little guilty, because *As a big sister, it's your job to take care of your brothers and not punch them in the arm and make them drop their new bikes in the snow and get them all wet* (this is a rule).

But, seriously, I have to walk Kevin to school *every day*. You would think Mark could do it *once*.

Finally, after what seemed like hours of waiting around with Erica telling me I shouldn't have punched Mark back and Kevin complaining he was hot in his snowsuit and couldn't we just get to school, Caroline and Sophie showed up, Sophie hobbling with her broken toe (there is nothing you can do for a broken toe. You just have to tape it to the toe next to it. We found this out after we waited three hours in the emergency room with Sophie's dad).

I ran to hug Caroline hello (not Sophie because I'd seen her every single day of Winter Break) and yelled, 'What's the Big News?'

'News?' Caroline looked confused. 'Sophie broke her toe. She said you were there when it happened.'

'She was there,' Sophie said. 'And she said it was only dislocated, and she tried to put it back in the socket. She said she knows about these things because she wants to be a vet. But it wasn't dislocated. It was broken, and it really hurt, and now there's a giant purple and green bruise, and my dad says—'

'No,' I interrupted. Sometimes Sophie exaggerates a little. But it's OK because she's the most beautiful girl in our class, so it's pretty easy to forgive her. 'I mean the news that you were going to tell Erica last night at the airport before your dad dragged you away.'

'Oh.' Caroline looked confused. 'Right. That. My dad said he saw Mrs Hunter in the grocery store over Winter Break and that she said we're getting a new student in our class this semester.'

Rule #2

It's OK to Lie If the Lie Makes
Someone Else Feel Better

It was really hard not to let my disappointment show.
While I was glad that Caroline wasn't moving away
or anything, I was sad that Caroline wasn't getting
her own reality show, or that her family hadn't won
the lottery.

Also, a new student wasn't all that exciting.

'Is that all?' I asked as Erica and I each took one
of Sophie's arms and helped her down the sidewalk
towards school, while Kevin waddled like a penguin
in his snowsuit towards the jungle gym, where the
other snowsuited kindergarteners were gathered.

'Yeah,' Caroline said. 'Well, except that the new
student is a girl.'

'Hey, this is good news,' Erica said. 'Now *you* won't
be the New Girl any more, Allie.'

This *was* good news and it cheered me up a little.

At least now someone else would have the curse of being new.

'That's true,' I said. Except this was still pretty boring news, compared to getting a horse for Christmas.

'And she's from Canada,' Caroline added.

I brightened up when I heard this. The new girl was from Canada! This was VERY exciting! I had never met anyone from Canada before. Canada was a whole different country. Canada was almost as far away as France, except that France was across the ocean. Well, maybe parts of Canada were too. Maybe the new girl could show us where us she was from on the big pull-down map that hung over the chalkboard in front of the classroom, which Mrs Hunter sometimes used to show us where we were in relation to other parts of America. Only this time we could see where we were in relation to where the new girl was from.

Just thinking about this made me so excited that I started walking too fast and Sophie complained. So I had to slow right down.

Even though a fresh layer of snow had fallen over Winter Break and should have made the playground white and wintry, enough kids had already gotten to school so that the snow was already dirty and messed up. This was pretty disappointing . . .

. . . but not as disappointing as the fact that even though I looked everywhere, I couldn't see the new girl anywhere!

Not that I know everyone in the whole school (I don't).

But I didn't see anyone who seemed as if she might be from Canada.

While I was standing there looking around, Mrs Hunter came hurrying past us from the teachers' parking lot.

'Oh, hello, girls,' she said. 'Happy New Year!'

'Hello, Mrs Hunter,' we said. I don't know about Caroline, Sophie or Erica, but I was feeling kind of shy from not having seen Mrs Hunter in so long. Plus, she was looking especially pretty in her dark green winter coat with the belt tightly waisted, with her hair curling all around her big imitation fur-trimmed collar.

'Oh, Allie,' Mrs Hunter said, looking right at me. *Me!* 'I'm glad I caught you before school. There's something important I need to ask you. Could you stop by my desk after you hang up your coat this morning?'

'Yes, of course,' I said. I was so completely shocked

by this request, it didn't occur to me to say anything else. Besides, what else are you going to say when your favourite teacher of all time asks you to do something? *No way?* I don't think so.

'Oh my gosh,' Erica said when Mrs Hunter had hurried away, her high-heeled boots crunching on the salt Mr Elkhart had sprinkled on the path. She headed towards the flagpole, where a group of teachers were standing, and hurried to join them. 'What do you think she wants?'

It was possible that Mrs Hunter had noticed my new fringed suede tote, and was going to ask where I got it. You never knew.

'I don't know,' I said. I didn't want to say anything in front of the other girls in case it made them jealous or something, but on reflection I was pretty sure Mrs Hunter was probably going to tell me how much she'd missed me over the holiday. I had overheard her mentioning to my grandmother once that I am a joy to have in the classroom. Who wouldn't miss having a joy like me around?

Well, except maybe the people in my family who were sick of listening to Dance Party America. But Mrs Hunter had never even been to my house.

'I hope it's nothing bad,' Erica said worriedly.

But what could it be that was bad?

As soon as Erica said that though, I started thinking about all the bad things Mrs Hunter might want to say to me in private at her desk. Like, what if before Winter Break I'd suddenly started getting bad grades or something? I was pretty sure I hadn't.

But what if I had?

Or – and this thought was even worse – what if Mrs Hunter was kicking me out of her class to make way for the new girl from Canada?

She couldn't do that. Could she?

'Of course it's nothing bad,' Sophie said. 'It's probably something great, like you're so smart they're bumping you up to the fifth grade!'

Except that this wouldn't be great. This would be the same as them kicking me out of class to make way for the new girl from Canada. Because I wouldn't be in the same class as my best friends forever, Sophie, Caroline and Erica.

'You probably won something,' Caroline said. Caroline is the smartest girl in both fourth-grade classes at Pine Heights Elementary combined, so she would know. She's always winning things. 'The last time Mrs Hunter had me stop by her desk before class started, it turned out she'd submitted an essay I'd written to a contest, and she'd wanted to let me know I'd won.'

'Oh, wow,' Erica said. 'Really? That would be

great, Allie, if Mrs Hunter was letting you know you'd won something!'

I perked up. If it was something like that, it *would* be great. Except I wasn't the greatest essay writer in the world. Math and science, maybe. Because math and science have rules, and I'm very good at following rules. But writing essays? Not so much.

'Ooooh,' Sophie said, clapping her mittened hands, her sore toe forgotten in her excitement, 'I know why she wants to see you! She wants you to be the person to officially show the new girl from Canada around!'

Erica sucked in her breath. 'I bet that's it! Oh, Sophie, you're so smart!'

'I know,' Sophie said modestly.

I thought about what Sophie said. It actually made sense. I mean, why not? I was the second newest person in the fourth grade at Pine Heights Elementary, after all. Who better to show the first newest person around the school?

Also, I knew Mrs Hunter liked me. I was a joy, anyway. Not to be a braggart or anything.

Sophie had to be right: I was going to be Mrs Hunter's helper for the new girl from Canada!

It was right after this that Sophie started pouting.

'How come Mrs Hunter didn't say anything about my foot?'

Even though the hospital had only taped Sophie's broken toe to the healthy toe next to it, instead of putting it in a cast, they'd given her a giant bootee to wear over it, as a sort of consolation prize. Sophie had been hoping everyone would notice her giant bootee and ask what had happened. Especially Mrs Hunter.

'I'm sure she'll notice when you have trouble getting up the stairs,' Caroline said sympathetically.

I wasn't worried about Mrs Hunter not having noticed Sophie's broken toe though. I was too excited about my new job as official show-arounder of the new girl from Canada.

Except that, when we went to stand in our lines to go inside, I looked all up and down the line and I didn't see any sign of the new girl.

Oh well, I thought to myself. Maybe she wasn't starting today. Sometimes new people didn't start on the exact day of the new semester. I had been new, and I hadn't.

It took us a while to get up to Room 209, our classroom, because Caroline and Erica and I had to help Sophie up the stairs due to her broken toe (Mrs Hunter did notice. She said, 'Sophie! What on earth happened?' and Sophie said, 'I broke my toe playing Olympic figure skater with Allie over Winter Break.'

'Oh dear,' Mrs Hunter cried. 'I hope it feels better soon!' This made Sophie beam with happiness. Although Mrs Hunter never did notice my new fringed suede tote).

After we finally reached the classroom (it seemed like it took forever) and I hung up my coat, I went up to Mrs Hunter's desk, where she was sitting. It was funny, but I felt shy again. Mrs Hunter was going over her lesson plans for the day. When she saw me coming, she looked up with a smile. Mrs Hunter has the nicest smile of any teacher I've ever seen. That's because she's so pretty. Also because she always makes sure to reapply her lipgloss (Clinique Full Potential Lips Plump and Shine . . . she showed me one time when I saw her putting it on and asked her what it was) whenever it rubs off.

'Oh, hello, Allie,' she said.

'Hi, Mrs Hunter,' I replied. I felt so shy I couldn't look Mrs Hunter in the eye. She has beautiful bright green eyes that could either twinkle with good humour or crackle with disapproval, depending on her mood. I had seen them crackling in disapproval at a couple of people who had misbehaved in class and, believe me, I did not want them ever crackling at me!

'Allie, I have a favour to ask you,' Mrs Hunter said, getting right down to business.

'Sure,' I said. So I hadn't won a contest after all. But that was OK. I hadn't expected that I had. At least if Mrs Hunter had a favour to ask, it didn't mean I'd done anything wrong, and that she was mad at me!

'We're going to be getting a new student today,' Mrs Hunter went on. 'She's a new girl, from Canada. Things are going to pretty strange for her here, and I know everyone is going to want to do everything they can to make her feel welcome. Don't you agree?'

I nodded my head so hard that my hair almost slid out of the new clip Mark had given me. I definitely wanted to make the new girl from Canada feel welcome. I knew *exactly* what it felt like to be the new girl.

'Good,' Mrs Hunter said. 'That's why, when I was trying to figure out where we were going to have her sit, it occurred to me that you might not mind giving up your seat next to Erica, and moving to the back row with Rosemary and Stuart and Joey and Patrick. I know you and Rosemary are friends now, and I think you'd be a very positive influence on those boys.'

I know it sounds weird, but the minute I heard what Mrs Hunter wanted me to do to help the new girl – give up my nice desk next to Erica, and move to the back row to sit by those nasty boys – my eyes filled up with tears.

I didn't want to sit next to Stuart Maxwell, who by the way likes to draw pictures of zombies eating other zombies' brains. I didn't want to go anywhere near Joey Fields, who never remembers to wash the sleep out of his eyes in the morning, and who likes to bark and growl like a dog instead of talking like a normal human person.

And Patrick Day likes to jump on top of his desk and pretend he is playing an air guitar every time Mrs Hunter leaves the room, screaming the words to whatever song is the number one country music hit that week. Rosemary has to pull him down and tell him he's not actually all that at least once *every single day*.

I don't want to sit by those boys! I don't want to sit anywhere near them!

But now it looked like I was going to have to. Because Mrs Hunter asked me especially. And she smiled when she asked, and said she thought I'd be a positive influence.

Which basically meant she thought I'd be just as

good as Rosemary at pulling Patrick down off his desk.

I didn't want to say yes. But I didn't really think Mrs Hunter had given me much of a choice. If I said, 'No. No, actually, I don't want to move to the back row with Rosemary and those crazy, bad boys,' I would just look like a really selfish person, and that wouldn't help the new girl at all.

And then Mrs Hunter wouldn't think I was joy to have around the classroom any more.

And I knew how hard it was to be new. I knew better than anybody.

So I said, hoping my tears weren't showing, 'Sure, I don't mind moving.' Even though this was a complete and total lie.

It's OK to lie if the lie makes someone else feel better. That's a rule.

Mrs Hunter smiled at me really big when I said this and went, 'Oh, thank you, Allie. I knew I could count on you. I've already had Mr Elkhart set up a desk for you between Stuart and Joey. Would you mind moving your things now? Because Cheyenne will be coming any minute.'

Cheyenne? Who was Cheyenne?

Then I realized Cheyenne must be the new girl. The new girl who was coming from Canada to take my perfectly nice old desk next to Erica, forcing me to sit between disgusting, zombie-drawing Stuart and sleep-encrusted-eyed, barking Joey.

I wanted to throw up. That's how grossed out I felt by what was happening to me.

Actually, I didn't even want to throw up. The truth was, I wanted to cry.

But I knew I couldn't be a baby about it and cry in front of Mrs Hunter, who was so nice, and told my grandma I was a joy to have around the classroom. Joys don't cry just because they have to move to sit between two boys. Even two disgusting, totally gross boys who don't wash.

So I said, giving Mrs Hunter the bravest smile I could manage, 'Sure, no problem.'

Rule #3

**Wearing the Fact That You Are Talented
on Your T-shirt Is Always a Smart Move**

Saying, 'Sure, no problem,' to Mrs Hunter was basically the hardest thing I had ever had to do in my
entire life.

I don't even know how I made my way to my desk,
there were so many tears in my eyes over the fact that
I was going to have to move to the back of the room
to sit by Stuart and Joey. But somehow I managed. As
I opened the lid of my desk and started taking my
stuff out, Erica asked, looking concerned, 'Allie,
what are you doing?'

'I'm moving,' I whispered. I had to whisper
because I was afraid if I started talking in a normal
voice I'd cry for real. 'To the back of the room. To
make way for the new girl. Her name is Cheyenne.'

'What?' Erica looked like *she* was about to cry

when she heard that. 'No. *That's* what Mrs Hunter wanted to see you about?'

Caroline and Sophie, who sit in the row in front of us, overheard and came rushing right over. Well, Caroline did. Sophie had to hobble.

'What? Oh my goodness, no!' Sophie's big brown eyes filled up with tears just like mine. Only, because it was Sophie, hers did it even more dramatically. 'That's not fair! You have to sit at the back? With Rosemary? And those *boys*?'

'It won't be so bad,' I tried to assure her, even though of course I knew it would. I'm not positive, but I'm pretty sure Patrick Day picks his nose. I don't think he eats it, but there's always a chance. 'I'll still see you guys at recess. And lunch, of course.'

'I think it's nice of Allie to move,' Caroline said after a moment of stunned silence. 'To let the new girl have a chance to sit near the front.'

Though truthfully, judging by her expression, it didn't seem as if she really believed what was happening was such a good thing. Probably she was thinking the same thing I was, about Patrick and his nostrils.

'Yeah,' I said. 'I'm letting the new girl have a chance to sit near the front.'

Except of course I wasn't really. I was just doing

what Mrs Hunter had asked me to do. It wasn't like I could have said no. Well, I could have, I guess. But then Mrs Hunter wouldn't have considered me a joy any more.

Erica's eyes were full of tears too, I noticed, as she and Caroline and Sophie helped me gather all my things out of my desk.

'I don't want to sit by some new girl,' Erica whispered to me. 'I mean, I'm sure she's very nice.' Erica hardly ever said mean things about other people, especially people she hadn't even met yet. She tried to get along with everyone, and to make everyone else get along as well. 'But I'm going to miss you so much!'

'I know,' I said, my chin starting to tremble. But I forced it to stop. 'But I know you'll like Cheyenne.' Actually – and this was a little bit selfish of me – I really hoped she *wouldn't* like Cheyenne. At least, not better than she liked me.

When Rosemary saw me coming towards the last row where she sat with the boys, her face brightened up like a Christmas tree that had just been plugged in.

'Oh my gosh, Allie,' she cried. 'Are you moving back here?'

'I sure am,' I said, trying to give her a big smile

while at the same glowering at the three boys, who groaned at the sight of me.

'Oh no,' Stuart cried. 'Not *her*!'

'Anyone but Finkle!' Patrick yelled.

'Boys,' Mrs Hunter said in her most disapproving voice. She'd stood up behind her desk, which was at the back of the room close to the last row, where I'd now be sitting (she'd put Stuart, Patrick and Joey back there so she could keep an eye on them from her desk – further proof they were the worst boys in the whole class). 'Allie is going to be sitting with you from now on, and I expect you to show her the same courtesy you show Rosemary.'

'Yeah,' I said, narrowing my eyes at them. 'Because if you don't, you'll be sorry.'

I'm not scared of boys. That's because I have little brothers, and I know that when it comes to a fight with boys, basically, they are just going to hit you, you're going to hit them back, and then it will be over.

Girls, on the other hand, scare me sometimes. Not girls like Erica or Caroline or Sophie, but other girls. That's because girls don't fight like boys. Girls use what my Uncle Jay calls psychological warfare. This is when they TELL you they're going to hit you but they don't say WHEN, so you are living in constant fear of being hit.

Or they will just not speak to you at all, or instead talk about you behind your back or even call you mean names to your face, which in some ways is almost worse than being hit. At least when you get hit, you get it over with.

With girls, it can just go on and on and on and on and on . . .

'Here you go, Allie,' Joey Fields said, holding open the top of my new desk, which was right next to his. 'Ruff, ruff, grrrrr!'

'Oh my goodness,' Sophie said faintly, staring at him. I had to take all my things out of her hands, because I was afraid she'd drop them in her alarm.

'Joey,' Rosemary yelled at him. 'Cut it out with the dog stuff. Allie,' she said to me. 'Didja see what I got for Christmas?' She showed me the brand-new cellphone she was holding, the buttons of which she was swiftly pressing. 'Check it out. It's got every game you can imagine. I can even make little movies. I want to make one of Mewsie. Can I go home with you for lunch today and make one? Please?'

I couldn't believe Rosemary got a cellphone for Christmas. A cellphone that made movies. And all I got was a wrap-around ballet sweater. And some

Boxcar Children books. And a hairclip and cherry ChapStick and a fringed suede tote. And OK, a PlayStation with Dance Party America. But I have to share that with my whole family.

'You better not let Mrs Hunter see that,' Erica warned Rosemary with a nervous look in Mrs Hunter's direction. 'It might end up in her drawer.'

Mrs Hunter has a special drawer in which she keeps an entire collection of confiscated electronic items, including Game Boys, cellphones, iPods, cameras, walkie-talkies and a vast assortment of radio-controlled vehicles, none of which she allows in her classroom. Once she confiscates them, she gives them back at the end of the week . . . *if* their owners behave.

'Oh, right,' Rosemary said, and hid her new phone in her pocket.

'If you're going to sit over here,' Stuart Maxwell said to me, 'you better be ready to face brain-eating zombies.' He held up a particularly grotesque drawing of a pair of zombies that were doing just that. He apparently did this in an effort to make me go sit somewhere else. Like I had a choice.

'Nice try,' I said, dumping all my stuff into the empty desk next to his. I'd arrange it nicely later. 'But I could draw better zombies than that in my sleep.'

'Oh yeah?' Stuart looked offended. 'With maggots coming out of their eyes?'

'Maggots,' I said, shutting the top of my desk, '*and* slime.'

'You're disgusting,' Stuart said to me. He looked over my shoulder at Joey Fields. 'She's disgusting.'

'Ruff,' Joey said, his eyes sparkling behind the sleep. 'Arf!'

I turned my head to look at him. 'Seriously,' I said. 'Shut up.'

'Oh.' Sophie looked like she was about to faint. Sophie, besides being the most beautiful girl in our class, is also just about the most girlie. 'Allie. Are you sure you're going to be all right back here?'

'She'll be fine,' Caroline said, handing over my pencil box and some of my books. She sounded heartier than she looked though. 'Won't you, Allie?'

'I'll be fine,' I assured them. I knew I would be. The boys didn't scare me. Even though I could see that Patrick was edging closer and closer to the top of his desk, getting ready to make a leap to do some air guitar. He didn't dare though, because Mrs Hunter was still in the room. She'd just gone to the front of the classroom in response to a knock on the door.

'I'll see you guys at recess,' I said to Sophie, Caroline and Erica, closing my desktop. 'It will be OK.' It was a little bit weird that I was the one telling them it was going to be OK, when the truth was, *I* could have used some reassurance.

Then Mrs Hunter was saying, 'Everyone to your seat, please!' and Caroline, Erica and Sophie were scurrying away, and I sank down into my new chair, thinking how far away the chalkboard seemed from back here, and how weird it was to be looking at the back of Erica's head instead of the side of her face, like usual.

As if *that* wasn't enough to make it sink in how much things were changing all around me, Stuart Maxwell whispered, 'Finkle. What about this one? This one scare you?' while holding up a new zombie drawing under his desk, and Joey Fields kept going, 'Grrrrr. Ruff. Arf,' beneath his breath, just to annoy me. I had to mutter, 'Quit it. Both of you,' to them, while wondering how on earth Rosemary had ever stood it back here for so long by herself.

And then Mrs Hunter pulled someone into the room from the hallway and said, 'Class, I'd like to introduce you to your new classmate, Cheyenne O'Malley. Cheyenne comes all the way from Ontario, Canada, so I'd like all of you to be extra nice to her, because this is her first time in our country.'

I sat up straighter in my seat so I could get a look

at Cheyenne. I had never seen anyone from Canada before (that I knew of).

And I wasn't disappointed either. Cheyenne was almost as beautiful as Sophie, and maybe even girlier, with her long curly dark hair held back in a single sparkly clip shaped like a flower, and a long-sleeved shirt that had the letters TNT on the front, with a picture of an explosion on it. Underneath the explosion, it said that TNT stood for *Talent, Not Talk*.

This was very clever, I realized, because by wearing that shirt Cheyenne was letting the whole class know right away that although she was very talented, she didn't have to talk about it.

I wished I had been smart enough to wear a shirt like that on my first day at Pine Heights Elementary.

Besides the shirt, Cheyenne was also wearing a denim miniskirt with brown suede high-heeled zip-upboots, which were exactly like the kind I'd asked for for Christmas but hadn't received, because my mom said I'm too young for high-heeled zip-up boots, and that I'd turn my ankle in them anyway. Instead, I'd gotten the fringed suede tote bag.

Cheyenne's mom obviously didn't feel the same way about high-heeled zip-up boots as my mom did. Cheyenne clearly had the nicest mom in the whole world.

Or else she just had very strong ankles.

'Cheyenne,' Mrs Hunter said. 'Would you like to tell the class a little bit about yourself?'

'Certainly, Mrs Hunter,' Cheyenne said, not looking at all nervous the way I had on my first day, when Mrs Hunter had asked me to tell the class a little bit about myself. She smiled at the class and said, 'Well, like your teacher said, my name is Cheyenne and I come from Toronto, which is the capital of Ontario, which is a province of Canada that borders the American states of Michigan, Ohio, New York, Pennsylvania and Minnesota. So I actually know quite a lot about American culture, and I've even watched most of your TV shows and eaten in the majority of your fast food restaurants before. Toronto is the largest city in Canada – it's *way* bigger than this town. In Toronto, my parents and I live in an apartment in a high-rise building, but here we're renting a house while my father is on sabbatical working on his book. His book is about American politics. He's considered an international expert on the subject.'

'Well,' Mrs Hunter said when Cheyenne stopped speaking and looked over at her expectantly, 'that's very interesting. We've learned a lot about Toronto and your father. But we haven't learned very much about you, Cheyenne. Is there anything you'd like us to know about you?'

I remembered when Mrs Hunter had asked me this in front of the whole class on *my* first day and how nervous I'd gotten. My knees had started to shake and I'd wanted to die on the spot. I felt sorry for Cheyenne, wondering if she felt the same way. I hoped if her knees started shaking, her ankles wouldn't turn in her high-heeled boots.

But if she felt nervous, you couldn't tell at all.

'Certainly,' Cheyenne said. 'I'm considered highly intelligent, and I enjoy water sports such as swimming and sailing, especially on Lake Ontario.'

'Thank you, Cheyenne,' Mrs Hunter said, before any of us had a chance to applaud. Well, I don't know if anyone but me felt like clapping. But I thought a speech that good deserved some applause. Cheyenne hadn't said 'um' once! 'You may take your seat. Your desk is right next to Erica Harrington . . . Erica, will you show her?'

Erica waved her arms to show Cheyenne where her (or really my) desk was. Cheyenne smiled graciously and went to sit down at her new desk. I watched as Erica said hello to her and helped her put away her things. All the things Cheyenne owned were very grown-up looking. For instance, her pencil box didn't have Hello Kitty, Webkinz or Bratz on it. It was just plain.

Which actually seemed kind of boring to me, but whatever. If I was starting a new school in a new country, I'd have gotten horses on *everything*. Or at the very least, rainbows or unicorns.

I saw that Caroline and Sophie had turned around in their seats in front of Erica's row to say hello. So had some of the other girls. Cheyenne, I could tell, was going to be popular. Probably because of her T-shirt. Who wouldn't want to be friends with someone who was all talent and no talk?

Wearing the fact that you are talented on your T-shirt is always a smart move. This is a rule.

I was going to have to wait until recess to talk to her, of course. Because I was stuck at the back with Rosemary and the Terror Triplets. There was no way I could even throw Cheyenne a special *Welcome to Pine Heights* note from here. It would never reach her. I was stuck at the back of Mrs Hunter's fourth-grade class, with the nose-pickers and the zombie brain-eaters.

Who knew if I'd ever even make it out alive?

Rule #4

Friendly People Don't Tell Other People That Their Games Are Babyish

I made it out for morning recess, but barely. I had to tell Stuart to knock it off with the zombie drawing four times. Finally I realized the only way he was going to stop showing me his disgusting horror sketches was to make my own, one that was so much grosser than his that he'd realize I was the Queen of the Zombie Drawings. I had to spend all math on mine, so I didn't raise my hand once, and let Caroline do all the answering, which I knew was unusual for me, and Mrs Hunter noticed.

She didn't say anything though. She must have known I was getting acclimatized to my new environment (I learned that expression in the animal books I like to read).

I showed my drawing to Stuart just before recess.

He was so freaked out he could barely speak, except to go, 'You didn't draw that . . . did you?'

So then I showed him my signature, *Allison Finkle*, at the bottom. Also that the fly pupae coming out of the skull's eyeballs were of my own creation. I'd gotten the idea for them from a dead squirrel I saw once.

I am naturally a very talented person.

The thing is, I have to talk about it, because I don't have a T-shirt to tell people about it.

As I was rushing to the coat-rack to get my coat and hat and stuff to go to recess, I saw a weird thing inside Joey Fields's desk. Or at least I thought I did. It was only out of the corner of my eye, so I can't be sure. But I thought I saw some of Mrs Hunter's old copies of the Boxcar Children inside his desk.

Except that isn't possible, because boys don't read those books. Especially weird bad boys like Joey Fields.

Of all the people in our classroom, the last person I'd suspect of being the one to selfishly hoard Mrs Hunter's Boxcar Children books for him or herself was Joey Fields. In my dazed state after trying to out-gross Stuart Maxwell, I must have been seeing things.

Once I was out in the playground with Erica,

Sophie and Caroline, I started feeling a bit better. Maybe it was the fresh air, even if it *was* cold.

Or maybe it was just being away from all those boys.

'Oh my gosh,' Erica said, hugging me. 'I miss you so much, Allie! It's so horrible, not sitting next to you! I wanted to say a million things to you all morning, and I kept turning my head to do it, only it wasn't you! It was that Cheyenne girl!'

'Mrs Hunter is probably happy you two are separated,' Caroline said knowingly. 'She hasn't mentioned the words chit-chat all day. It's a new world record.'

'You don't think she moved Allie on purpose because of that,' Sophie cried. 'Do you?'

'No,' Caroline said. 'Although I did notice there were a lot fewer disturbances from the back today. Allie seems to be having a good influence on those boys. How are you handling things back there, Allie?'

I made a face. 'Let's not talk about it,' I said. 'I just want to forget about the back row for fifteen minutes. Let's go play queens, OK?'

'I thought you'd never ask,' Erica said with a smile, and took my hand. We were about to run across the playground together when Erica stopped dead and I nearly ran into her. Which made Sophie almost hobble into me, and Caroline almost run into her.

'What?' Caroline asked. 'What is it?'

'You guys,' Erica said. 'Look.'

Erica pointed. It was kind of hard to see what she was pointing at because she was wearing mittens. But we looked in the general direction of where her arm was waving, and saw the saddest thing. Which was Cheyenne sitting all by herself on one of the swings. The swings were pretty much deserted because it was the middle of winter and too cold to go swinging (we'd tried it once and ended up getting snot on our faces).

Cheyenne must have known about this since she wasn't swinging. She was just sitting there, staring down at her feet. No one was talking to her and she wasn't talking to anybody else.

'Awwww,' Sophie said. 'The poor thing.'

'Should we ask her to play?' Erica wanted to know.

'Mrs Hunter would want us to,' I said. I was sure of that.

'Should we ask her to play queens?' Caroline sounded as if she didn't think so.

'Well,' I said, 'she *is* talented.'

'How do you know?' Caroline asked.

'Because,' I said, 'her shirt says so.'

'Anyone could buy that shirt,' Caroline pointed out intelligently.

'Yes,' I said. Actually, I hadn't thought of that. 'But most people wouldn't unless they really were talented.'

'That's true,' Sophie said. 'Who would want to walk around with a big lie on their chest?'

Caroline looked at Erica. 'You've sat next to her all morning. Do you think she'd like playing queens?'

Erica shrugged. 'Who wouldn't? Well . . . except Rosemary.'

This was true.

'Oh well,' Caroline said, giving a little shrug of her own. 'We're just going to have to find out for ourselves. Come on.'

So we all ran over to where Cheyenne was sitting, and said, 'Hi!' and, 'Hello, Cheyenne!' and, 'Do you want to play with us?'

To my surprise, however, instead of looking up gratefully and saying, *Oh, thank you for coming over to me when no one else on the whole playground would*, the way I expected her to, Cheyenne said very briskly, 'That depends. What game are you playing?'

'We like to play a game we call queens,' Caroline explained, because she is the champion speller of our school, so we usually let her do all the talking. 'We pretend that we're four queens, and that an evil war-lord is trying to force Sophie to marry him, only she doesn't want to marry him because her heart belongs to another, Peter Jacobs – he's over there in the green coat, playing kickball.' Caroline helpfully pointed Peter out. 'He's in Mrs Danielson's fourth-grade class next door—'

'You guys!' Sophie squealed, blushing with embarrassment. But you could tell she liked the attention.

'So we have to fight the evil warlord with swords and truncheons and boiling oil and stuff,' Caroline went on. 'We play it in this cool wooded area over there.' Caroline pointed at the secret fort where we usually play queens. 'Anyway, you can come over and play with us, if you want.'

Cheyenne looked over at where Caroline was pointing. Then she smiled politely and said, not getting up from her swing, 'No thank you. Actually, I don't know whether or not you noticed, but we're in the fourth grade. That's a little old for playing such babyish games of let's pretend, don't you think?'

I was so shocked I didn't know what to say or do. I couldn't believe she'd actually said that – that our game was babyish. I just stood there staring at her until I felt someone's hand on my arm and heard

Caroline going, 'Well, I'm very sorry you feel that way. We'll leave you alone now. Bye,' and realized Caroline was pulling me away.

'Oh my goodness, oh my goodness,' Sophie was saying, over and over, as Caroline dragged the three of us away from the swings. 'Did you hear what she said? Did you hear? She did not just say that. She did *not!*'

'She didn't mean it,' Erica was saying, because Erica can't believe anyone would ever say anything mean. 'Maybe she misunderstood, because she's from another country. Why would she say such a mean thing?'

'Of course she meant it,' Caroline said. I had never seen Caroline so mad. There was practically steam coming out of her ears, she was so angry. She was practically stomping towards the bushes that guarded the secret entrance to our private fort where we played queens. 'Just because we like to play our own made-up games instead of whatever it is *she* likes to play. Which is apparently nothing. Apparently all *she* likes to do is sit and stare into space.'

'Well . . .' Erica looked over her shoulder at Cheyenne. 'Maybe she doesn't know any better.'

'Some people have no *manners*,' Caroline said.

'Come on, you guys, let's forget about her and just play.'

We ducked beneath the bushes and went inside our secret castle and played a nice round of queens, forgetting all about Cheyenne O'Malley.

Or at least, we tried. Well, I tried.

But it was sort of hard to concentrate when I kept hearing Cheyenne's voice in my head, saying, *Actually, I don't know whether or not you noticed, but we're in the fourth grade. That's a little old for playing such babyish games of let's pretend, don't you think?*

I don't know if the other girls were hearing that same voice in their heads or not.

But I do know for me it was awful! Was fourth grade too old for games of let's pretend? Caroline, Sophie, Erica and I played let's pretend games all the time. We pretended we were queens. We pretended we were space-shuttle captains (a game I borrowed from my brothers who played space shuttle all the time with the radiator between their rooms. But I would never, ever tell them I'd gotten the idea from them. And we didn't use the stupid radiator when we played). We played pretend with our AmericanGirl dolls (well, not Caroline because she didn't have one, but she used Erica's extra ones). Sometimes we pretended we were in high school and got dressed up like teenagers in Erica's sister Missy's stuff (and then had to deal with Missy's anger when she found out and we got caught. But it was totally worth it). Sometimes we played mad scientist and mixed together all the different cleaners we found under the kitchen sink in Caroline's house to see if they would explode. Sometimes we pretended we were movie stars and dressed up in Sophie's mom's stuff (and then had to deal with Sophie's mom's anger when we got caught. But it was also totally worth it).

Was that babyish?

Maybe it was.

But it was also totally fun! I mean, if dressing up in someone else's mom's clothes and make-up is babyish, well, then I didn't want to be grown up.

When the warning bell rang, letting us know it was time to line up to go back inside, I don't think I was the only one who didn't think recess had been quite long enough to get over the trauma of the morning.

But we came out of the bushes and hurried to get into our lines to go back inside anyway. As we did, I noticed that Cheyenne wasn't by herself any more. She was walking with Marianne and Dominique, two girls from our class.

'Oh look,' Erica said. 'Cheyenne found some

friends. Now we don't have to worry about her any more.'

'Who's worrying about her? Not me,' I said.

'You don't think she's telling them what you said about Prince Peter, do you, Caroline?' Sophie asked worriedly. Sophie's crush on Peter was a secret, but it was a secret we talked about so much that we sometimes forgot it was a secret.

'No,' Caroline said. 'Why would she do that? That would just be malicious.'

Being the champion speller of our school – but not of our district, Caroline had been beaten out by a girl from a rival elementary school in the district championship last month – Caroline sometimes used big words we didn't understand. But I knew what malicious meant.

I couldn't tell yet if Cheyenne was malicious or not. I hadn't really known her long enough. One thing I did know was, she wasn't all that friendly. *Friendly people don't tell other people that their games are babyish.* That's a rule.

But maybe Cheyenne was just having a bad day. We all do sometimes, especially on our first day at a new school in a new country. Probably we should give Cheyenne another chance. The fact was, she was most likely just scared and maybe a little nervous . . .

even though she hadn't seemed that way. She had seemed pretty confident actually.

Still, even the most confident people have bad days sometimes. Or at least, that's what I've been told by my mom, and people on TV.

So I wasn't going to start disliking Cheyenne yet, much less hating her (because *You aren't supposed to hate people.* That's a rule too. Even though of course there are a lot of people who deserve to be hated, such as murderers and people who are mean to animals on purpose). I was going to give her another chance.

Starting right after lunch.

I invited Rosemary, Caroline, Sophie and Erica over for lunch, mostly because I wanted them to try Dance Party America, but also because I wanted them to see how big Mewsie has gotten. Mom doesn't mind when I invite people over for lunch without telling her first, because I know how to make my own lunches now and she always buys extra food just in case I want to have people over. And when my mom doesn't have enough hot dog buns or whatever (microwave hot-dogs are always a big hit with my friends), we can go to Erica's, because Mrs Harrington always has tons of food, since Erica has a brother who is a teenager. I once saw John eat eight oranges in a row without stopping or even noticing he was doing it. He wouldn't have stopped either except that his mom made him because she said he was going to make himself sick.

But when we got to my house for lunch that first day back after Winter Break, I couldn't show my friends Dance Party America. That's because my Uncle Jay was lying on the couch in the TV room all wrapped up in a blanket watching the twenty-four-hour news channel, which we kids aren't supposed to watch, but Uncle Jay knows the password to the parental V-chip Mom installed (so do us kids actually, which is how Uncle Jay knows it, but we told him not to tell that we know it).

'What are *you* doing here?' I asked him. Uncle Jay lives in an apartment on campus, where he is a student.

'Hello,' Uncle Jay said, turning down the sound of the TV with the remote. 'That's a very gracious greeting.'

'Hi, Mr Finkle,' Caroline said. Caroline isn't very shy around adults. That's because of her cosmopolitan upbringing as the daughter of an East Asian studies professor. My dad just teaches computers. 'Are you not feeling well?'

'Please,' Uncle Jay said, not getting up from the

couch, 'call me Jay. Mr Finkle was my father. And no, I'm not feeling well.'

'Do you have a broken toe?' Sophie wanted to know. She showed him her Velcro bootee. 'I do too.'

'I don't have a broken toe,' Uncle Jay said. He didn't even raise his head up from the couch cushion. 'If only my problem was that simple.'

'Do you have the flu?' Erica asked. 'My sister, Missy, got it when we were in Florida last week. She threw up for three days straight.'

'I have been stricken,' Uncle Jay said, 'but not with a virus. And something about me is broken, but it's not my toe. It's my heart.'

By this time Kevin had finally peeled off his snowsuit and come into the room. He looked down at Uncle Jay on the couch and went, 'Are you going to die?'

'Death is inevitable,' Uncle Jay said.

Mark had also come into the room. He looked down at Uncle Jay and asked, 'If you die, can I have your Xbox?'

'Mark!' I cried. *Boys can seriously be so stupid sometimes. Also deeply thoughtless.* That's a rule.

'Of course you can,' Uncle Jay said, giving Mark a pat on the hand. 'I won't need it any more, where I'm going.'

'Jay.' I heard my mom's voice coming from her office, which is just off the utility room. 'Stop being so dramatic. Kids, leave Jay alone. He's having a bad day. His girlfriend just broke up with him, that's all.'

Rule #5

**Just Because Something Is Popular
Doesn't Mean It's Good**

I was shocked. Shocked to hear that my Uncle Jay's girlfriend, Harmony, had broken-up with him, and that Uncle Jay, in his depression over this, couldn't go back to his apartment, where the break-up had occurred, because the sight of it made him too sad.

Instead, he had to lie on our couch in the TV room watching CNN and eating microwave popcorn.

'But who's going to feed Wang Ba?'

Those were the first words out of my mouth. It maybe wasn't the most sympathetic thing to say.

But when you have rescued a turtle from a Chinese food restaurant where it was facing certain death, and your uncle has promised to take care of it, you too would ask who was going to feed it upon learning that your uncle had decided to live on your couch instead.

48

'Don't worry about Wang Ba,' Uncle Jay said with a sigh. 'My neighbour's promised to look in on him.'

'That's a relief,' I said.

Still. Uncle Jay did look terrible. He hadn't shaved in a while, and the goatee he'd been growing looked all crooked and awful.

It wasn't any wonder Harmony had broken up with him. He looked like something that had crawled out of the woods. And not in a cute, cuddly way.

'Kids,' Mom said, 'leave Uncle Jay alone. Come into the kitchen and have some soup. You can make yourselves some ham and cheese Hot Pockets too.'

Ham and cheese Hot Pockets happen to be one of my favourites, so I was very torn by this, of course. On the one hand I really wanted to eat. But on the other hand, I also really wanted to hear about Uncle Jay and his girlfriend.

So, it turned out, did Sophie.

'Harmony broke up with you?' Sophie cried. I forgot Sophie had met Uncle Jay's girlfriend when the two of them had babysat for us while my mom and dad had gone to a party given by some people in my mom's office, and Sophie had been at my house for a sleepover during Winter Break.

'She said it's clear we want different things out of life,' Uncle Jay explained. 'She said she wants a career, family and home ownership, while it's obvious all I want to do is be a perpetual student for the rest of my life. Which is true, but I don't see what's wrong with a thirst for knowledge. She also said it's clear from my refusal to find a job that I lack commitment. But I said, why should I, an artist, toil like the common man, and possibly lose my artistic soul?'

'Jay!' Mom yelled from the kitchen. 'This is not an appropriate conversation to be having with nine-year-olds. Kids! Get in here! Your soup is getting cold.'

'Uncle Jay,' Kevin said, 'if you die, can I have your futon couch?'

'Why do you want my futon?' Uncle Jay asked.

'So when people come upstairs to my room,' Kevin said, 'I can tell them, "Have a seat on my futon couch."'

'You can have my futon couch,' Uncle Jay said sadly, staring at the TV.

'I'm going to get a different cover for it though,' Kevin whispered to me as we were going back into the kitchen. 'Uncle Jay's futon cover is boring and ugly. It's just brown. I'm going to get a purple one. In velvet.'

'You're horrible,' I told Kevin. 'How can you think

about yourself at a time like this? And besides, Uncle Jay isn't going to die.'

Kevin said, 'He will if all he eats is popcorn.'

We all agreed it was hard to concentrate on eating lunch when in the other room there was a man possibly dying of a broken heart. I knew how much Uncle Jay loved Harmony, and that was a lot. Harmony was studying to be a television news reporter, and she was very beautiful, with long black hair, and delicate hands that fluttered around when she talked. She always seemed to know the right thing to say. One time she had written a story about me that had gotten into our town newspaper and made me a temporary celebrity.

'Your uncle should just say he's sorry,' Erica said as we ate our Hot Pockets and drank our soup. 'Then Harmony will forgive him and they can get married.'

'But he can't say he's sorry if he isn't really sorry,' Caroline pointed out. 'And if he doesn't plan on changing. That would be a lie. And Harmony would notice if he didn't get a job.'

'It's so sad,' Sophie said with a sigh. 'I can't eat, I'm so torn up about it. I've never seen a man in so much pain.'

'Let's go film Mewsie before we go back to school,' Rosemary said. Rosemary took a more practical view of things. And she was right. We couldn't do Dance Party America anyway, since Uncle Jay was hogging the TV. Besides, when we peeked in on him after rinsing our soup bowls and putting them in the dishwasher, he was snoring, the moustache of his goatee moving back and forth in the air with his breath. There were popcorn kernels in it.

'Ew,' Sophie said.

We spent so much time filming, petting and brushing Mewsie – he's a long-haired kitten, and so needs a lot of grooming, because his little tongue isn't big enough yet to comb through all his long, silky grey, white and black striped fur – that we barely got back to the playground in time for the end of lunch recess.

But when we did, we saw an extraordinary sight.

And that was Cheyenne, the new girl, leading a number of the girls from Room 209 and even some from Mrs Danielson's fourth-grade class next door in a brand-new game.

At first we couldn't figure out what the game was. It just seemed to involve a lot of girls running from one end of the playground to the other. It took us a little while to see that running in front of the girls was one solitary boy, who kept trying to duck behind other groups of kids in an attempt to hide from the girls.

This didn't seem to work, however, since the other groups of kids would get out of the way as soon as they saw the stampede of girls thundering towards them.

I didn't blame them. I'd get out of the way too.

It took another few seconds for us to recognize the identity of the boy who was running from the herd of girls.

'Um,' Caroline said, after a minute, 'Isn't that Prince Peter?'

Just at that moment my brother Mark strolled past us, holding the kickball from the game he'd been playing over on the baseball diamond, which had been disrupted when the girls had ripped through it. Mark was shaking his head in disgust.

'Who's that boy?' I grabbed Mark's arm and pointed. 'What are they doing to him?'

'That's Peter Jacobs.' Mark looked surprised that I was speaking to him. We have a policy of not acknowledging one another's presence in the play-ground. It's one of my rules.

'*What?*' All the colour drained from Sophie's face. Sophie is actually a very good actress. Sometimes when we play queens and we make out like Sophie gets the news that the evil warlord has decapitated Prince Peter, Sophie pretends to faint, and she does an excellent job of it. She can make her body completely rubbery.

But you could tell she wasn't acting now. She really did look like she was about to faint. I hurried to stand behind her so I could catch her if she fell over.

'Oh yeah,' Mark said, as we watched Peter finally bust his way out from amidst the girls, yelling, *Get away from me!* 'That new girl started it. The one from Canada. It's called the Kissing Game. She says everybody plays it, back where she comes from.' Seeing that we were looking at him blankly, Mark elaborated. 'Basically, the girls pick a boy and then they chase after him until they catch him. And then the new girl tries to kiss him.'

'I need to sit down,' Sophie said after a minute, looking like she really might faint after all.

'I know,' Mark said, nodding. He didn't understand what she meant. He didn't know about Sophie's crush on Peter. 'It makes me want to throw up too. Pete's our best pitcher.'

Rosemary nodded, agreeing with him. She didn't know about Sophie's crush on Prince Peter either. 'Those girls are insane. Have they no dignity?'

'Seriously,' Sophie said faintly. 'I need to sit down like now.'

We left Mark and Rosemary commiserating about the ruined kickball game and helped Sophie hobble towards the steps to the front of the school. Pine Heights Elementary is so old-fashioned that there are entrances with stone carved signs over them, one marked *Boys*, one marked *Girls*, but no one obeys what they say any more. We sat Sophie down in front of the sign marked *Boys* and encouraged her to stick her head between her knees, because I saw a paramedic tell a lady to do that on a TV show once. Sophie did it, but I could hear her crying a little. We were patting her on the back and telling her not to worry when I heard a familiar click-clack on the pavement and I looked up to see Mrs Hunter looking down at us with concern on her pretty, rosy-cheeked face.

'Girls,' Mrs Hunter said, 'is everything all right?'

'Oh, everything's just fine, Mrs Hunter,' Erica said quickly. We knew Sophie would sooner die than let Mrs Hunter know about her inner pain. 'Sophie, um . . . her, um . . .'

'Her broken toe just hurts,' Caroline said.

I was glad Caroline was such a quick thinker. I wouldn't have been able to think of something that fast. I was still remembering how Prince Peter's face had looked as all those girls had caught up with him. He'd seemed totally panicked.

'Oh dear,' Mrs Hunter said. 'Well, why don't you three go up the stairs now, ahead of everyone else, so Sophie gets a bit of a head start? That way she won't get crushed when the rest of us go up. Would that be all right, Sophie?'

Sophie lifted her tear-stained face and nodded, unable to speak in her grief.

'Th-thanks,' was all she was able to get out.

Mrs Hunter smiled again and went away. We got Sophie to her feet and started taking her inside.

'The thing is,' Sophie finally managed to burst out, when we were inside helping her up the stairs, and the warm air from the old-timey radiators was melting our frozen cheeks, 'she *knows*. She *knows* how I feel about him. Because Caroline told her. She's doing it on purpose.'

'Who knows?' Erica asked in bewilderment.

'The new girl,' Sophie said. 'That Cheyenne girl. She knows I love Peter.'

'Oh, Sophie,' Caroline said, just as Erica said, 'I'm sure she didn't do it on purpose.'

But I agreed with Sophie. I was sure she *did* do it

on purpose. The thing was, I had had some experience with girls like Cheyenne. I hoped I was wrong.

But I didn't think so.

And a few minutes later, when we'd gotten Sophie into her seat, and the bell rang and the rest of our class hurried back into the room, I heard enough to confirm that I was right – at least as far as I was concerned.

'Oh my gosh, that was so fun,' Dominique was saying as she hung up her coat.

'I know,' Marianne was gushing. 'I've *never* had that much fun at recess before.'

'That's the best game ever,' Shamira agreed. 'Who are you going to kiss at afternoon recess, Cheyenne?'

Cheyenne fluffed out her curly hair and looked around Room 209. Her gaze fell on Stuart Maxwell, innocently returning to his desk besides mine.

'Him,' she said simply.

'Oh, excellent,' Rosie Myers said, clapping her hands. 'He'll be easy to spot, because of his red hair.'

'Unless he's wearing a hat,' Elizabeth said.

I couldn't believe it! Even shy Elizabeth Pukowski, who never said anything to anyone (or at least, never to me), was in on the Kissing Game! How had this happened? And in just the short time between when we left for lunch and when we came back! How could we have gone from feeling sorry for Cheyenne to her ruling the school (well, practically)?

And how had the Kissing Game gotten so popular? *Just because something is popular doesn't mean it's good.* That's a rule. There were many examples of things that weren't good being popular, such as high-heeled zip-up boots. They could turn your ankle (at least according to my mom).

Also McDonald's. McDonald's tastes good, and of course everyone loves it, but if you eat it every day like I want to, you could have a heart attack and die.

And what about racing cars? Racing cars are very, very popular, but one of the reasons people like watching them is to see them crash. The problem is, when racing cars crash, the people driving them can get hurt. This is exciting for the people watching, but sometimes not so good for the people driving them.

These are just a few examples of popular things that aren't good for you. But of course there are many, many more.

It was amazing to me that Marianne, Dominique, Shamira, Rosie and Elizabeth couldn't see that Cheyenne's game wasn't any good, even though it might seem that way, like high-heeled zip-up boots,

McDonald's, and racing car driving. Any game that came from Canada might seem exciting and exotic.

But couldn't they see it had already made Sophie cry?

Well, maybe not.

Still, you would think they would have noticed how mad it had made Prince Peter. He hadn't looked too happy when he'd stalked away from that group of girls he'd been swallowed into earlier. He hadn't looked like he'd liked any of them – especially Cheyenne – too much. If getting boys to like them was the goal, why were they all doing something that just made boys hate them?

It didn't make any sense, if you asked me.

But then, no one *had* asked me.

I went to sit down next to Stuart, who wasn't paying the slightest bit of attention and had no idea what was about to befall him in one hour and twenty minutes, at afternoon recess. I thought that maybe, just to be fair, I should warn him.

I was kind of confused though. I was a girl, not a boy. Should I be on the girls' side, or the boys'?

I decided that, since I was a friend of Sophie's, I'd be on the boys' side.

'Ahem,' I said to Stuart.

'What?' Stuart demanded. 'I already said your zombie drawing was the grossest. Leave me alone.'

'No,' I said. 'That's not it.' How was I going to explain to him that at recess a whole lot of girls were going to chase him and then trap him into letting Cheyenne kiss him? Maybe he wouldn't mind this. I didn't know. Maybe I should just mind my own business.

'Then what?' Stuart wanted to know. 'I'm not doing anything to you, Finkle. Just Stinkle off.'

Well! So much for trying to do a person a favour! Let him get kissed by every girl in the entire fourth grade! See how he liked it!

'Fine,' I said. 'Don't I say I didn't warn you then.'

'Warn me about what?' Stuart asked suspiciously.

'You'll find out,' I said. 'When it's too late.'

On the other side of me, Joey was looking all around.

'Hey,' he said. 'Why are all the girls whispering together?'

'Not all of them,' I said. 'I'm not. Rosemary's not. Sophie and Caroline and Erica aren't. So your statement is not very accurate.'

'You guys aren't girls,' Joey said. 'Well, not *real* girls.'

I gave him a very dirty look. Now I felt less like

helping those boys than ever. I had only been sitting next to them for less than one day, and already I wasn't a real girl? And neither were my friends?

'Well, you know what I mean,' Joey said, looking a little bit sorry. But just a little bit. Then, because I just kept looking at him, he went, 'Ruff!' I noticed he always started barking when he was nervous.

'Just forget it,' I said in disgust. 'You guys deserve every bit of what you're about to get.'

And boy, did they ever get it.

Rule #6

Lying Doesn't Solve Anything
(Usually)

It didn't take long for the Kissing Game to become the rage of the fourth grade. Well, amongst most of the girls, anyway. The boys still had no idea what was going on. Until it was their turn to be chased, that is.

Then they found out pretty quickly.

If you asked me, they liked it. Well, OK, that's an exaggeration. Patrick Day liked it. Most of the rest of the boys didn't seem to. Most of the rest of the boys would run so fast when they saw that stampede of girls coming towards them, you would think their hair was on fire.

But Patrick Day would only run away from them for a little while – and not very fast either – before letting himself get caught. You could tell he liked it when Cheyenne leaned in and kissed him. He'd laugh and yell, 'Stop, stop – take it easy! There's enough of me to go around, you know, ladies!'

Whereas all the other boys would yell, furiously wipe their cheeks where she'd kissed them, and go, 'Get away from me! Gross! Cheyenne! That's sick!'

Caroline, Sophie, Erica and I, watching from the sidelines, just shook our heads and tried to figure out how all this had happened. Rosemary, whose recess kickball games were suffering from these constant interruptions – she never knew when one of her team members might turn out to be a target for Cheyenne – was less concerned with how it had happened and more concerned with making it stop.

'Maybe if I gave them all a fist sandwich,' she said, meaning Cheyenne and all the other girls involved.

'You can't,' I said to her. 'There are too many of them.'

'I'll stomp them,' Rosemary said. She looked like she meant it. 'Like the little rats they are!'

I was glad I wasn't one of those rats. But I also knew violence wasn't the answer, so I told Rosemary this.

'It's not our fight,' I explained. 'The boys are the victims. It's up to them to do something.'

'Oh, right,' Rosemary said, rolling her eyes. 'Like *that's* going to happen.'

I hated to say it, but it was looking like Rosemary was right. The boys were totally incapable of figuring out how to solve the problem – even though it was really bothering them (well, except Patrick Day). Stuart Maxwell told me in a shaky voice that the first time Cheyenne picked him out as her victim for the Kissing Game it had been like a nightmare, as he'd found himself cornered by the circle of girls, only to see Cheyenne's lips coming closer and closer to his cheek, until finally the smell of cranberry Kiehl's Lip Balm had overwhelmed him.

'And that's when,' Stuart told me in a horrified voice, 'I knew it was all over.'

'Well,' I said, 'you should have run faster.'

I maybe felt a little bit sorry for not having warned him about what was going to happen. But truthfully, I didn't have a whole lot of sympathy for him . . . or any of the boys. I mean, if they didn't want to get caught and kissed, there was something they could have done: Tell Mrs Hunter. She was always standing out there by the flagpole with the other teachers. I'd even seen her staring at the running girls with a slightly perplexed look on her pretty face, as if she was trying to figure out what was happening. Any boy who wanted to escape Cheyenne and her puckered lips could easily have run up to the teachers and asked them to make her stop.

I didn't understand why they didn't.

Although it might have been for the same reasons why I, when I was being threatened by a bully when I first started at Pine Heights Elementary, didn't want to tell my mom, for fear she'd tell Mrs Hunter: it might actually have made things worse.

If the Kissing Game was bad for the boys who got caught and kissed by Cheyenne (except for Patrick, who liked it), it seemed in some ways to be worse for the boys Cheyenne *didn't* seem interested in catching and kissing.

And one of those boys was Joey Fields.

I don't know what poor Joey did to make Cheyenne so uninterested in him. But she treated Joey like he had the chicken pox and poison ivy *combined*.

And this was bad, because Joey *wanted* to be kissed by Cheyenne. And *badly*. I knew this, because every day he bugged me about it. For some reason Joey thought I was in on the whole Kissing Game, and he kept asking me about it. Like, 'Allie, who are they going to chase at recess today?' and 'Do you think they'll chase me? I hope not! Ruff! Ruff!'

Except you could tell that underneath the *I hope*

nots and the nervous barking, Joey really hoped they *would* chase him. I could tell because he started bringing mints to school and sucking them all the time.

It was about as sad as it was gross.

Plus, he actually started washing the sleep out of his eyes every morning, and combing the sticky-out parts of his black hair down.

Also, he made an effort to separate himself from the rest of the guys on the playground, so he'd make an easy target for Cheyenne if she wanted to issue the command to start chasing him. Instead of playing kickball like he usually did, Joey started sitting by himself on the swings, reading a book. Or *pretending* to read a book, I should say. Really, he was just opening the book, while watching the girls to see if they were going to chase him or not.

This was how I became sure that my eyes hadn't been playing tricks on me that first day I'd moved to my new desk. Joey Fields really was the other kid in Room 209 who was reading Mrs Hunter's collection of Boxcar Children books. He was hoarding them all in his desk! I saw him with them out in the playground, and sometimes I saw him taking them home at night. I couldn't understand how a boy as weird as Joey could love the same kind of books that I did.

Also, I couldn't figure out how I could make him give them back. He had like ten of them in his desk. The one time I confronted him about it – 'Joey,' I said, in my most reasonable big sister voice (*Sometimes you have to use your reasonable voice to get what you want. Especially with boys.* This is a rule), 'why do you have all Mrs Hunter's Boxcar Children books in your desk? Those books are for everyone, you know. You're supposed to borrow them one at a time. Please put them back so all of us can enjoy them' – he denied that they were there, and tried to make out like I was seeing things. Liar!

Lying doesn't solve anything. Usually. This is a rule.

I understand that a boy like Joey might be ashamed to be caught reading the same books as a girl.

But still! He didn't have to lie about it.

I was little bit glad that Cheyenne didn't want to kiss Joey, even though you could tell he was totally miserable about it. I wouldn't have wanted to kiss him either (although the fact was, I didn't want to kiss any boy).

So there I was, stuck in the back row between a boy who was miserable because the new girl in our class wouldn't stop kissing him, and a boy who was miserable because the new girl in our class didn't want to kiss him.

This was just living proof of what my Uncle Jay was saying a lot lately, about how there was no just-ice in the world.

I was pretty mad about it. Especially since I had innocently been taking a drink from the water fountain (like everything in Pine Heights Elementary School, the water fountains are old-fashioned, not the kind with a pedal that you step on or a button that you push to make the water come out, but with a star-shaped cranky thing you turned) in the hall-way on our way to the choir room for music class, when Cheyenne got in line behind me (with Dominique and Marianne in line behind her), and asked, 'Drink much?' in a snotty voice, which I guess in Canadian meant I was taking too long or some-thing.

So I stopped drinking and turned around, wiping my mouth with the back of my wrist before I told Cheyenne to go stinkle somewhere else.

This caused Cheyenne to go, 'Way to drool!'

Then Dominique and Marianne laughed, exactly like they'd laughed when Cheyenne had asked, *Drink much?*

I just looked at Cheyenne some more, because I

was thinking that, actually, the shirt she'd been wearing her first day at school had turned out not to be telling the truth. She wasn't *Talent, Not Talk*. Cheyenne talked quite a lot, it turned out. She talked all the time. She was always getting caught chitchatting in class by Mrs Hunter, but never with her neighbour, Erica. She was always chit-chatting with Dominique, who sat behind her, or Marianne, who sat in front of her, or Shamira, who sat diagonally opposite her – when she wasn't passing notes to them.

Today she was wearing a long-sleeved shirt that had sparkles all over the front that formed the words *Girl Power!* Girl power, when it came to Cheyenne, was right. She had a little too *much* girl power, if you asked me.

'Well,' Cheyenne said to me, 'are you going to move, or what?'

I'd started to walk away because there didn't seem to be anything more to say, when the sound of Cheyenne's voice stopped me.

'Hey, Allie,' she said. 'How come you never want to play the Kissing Game with us at recess?'

I looked over my shoulder at her.

'Because I think the Kissing Game is stupid,' I said. 'Why would I want to chase after a boy so you could kiss him? Especially any of the boys from our class. They're gross.'

This caused Dominique and Marianne to erupt into even more giggles, as if this was the funniest thing they'd ever heard in their entire lives.

Cheyenne laughed too. 'Oh, Allie,' she said, 'you're so immature!'

I walked away when she said that, and kept walking, straight into the music room. I sat down next to Erica, Caroline and Sophie. I didn't say anything just then about what Cheyenne had accused me of, but I couldn't stop thinking about it.

Was I immature? I didn't think so. I actually thought I was quite mature for my age. Unlike some girls I know, I don't cry at the drop of a hat just because I don't get my way. I had nursed a premature kitten to health all by myself (practically), and I was one of the top spellers and the best girl in math and science (besides Caroline) in our entire class. I also took very good care of my little brothers (most of the time), and even of my Uncle Jay now that he had pretty much moved into our house due to his depression over his girlfriend breaking up with him. Weren't these actually signs of great maturity? Yes, I think they were.

Cheyenne may have been from a big city in

Canada, but that didn't mean she knew what she was talking about. Just because a person didn't want to run around the playground like a maniac, chasing boys and then kissing them, did not mean a person wasn't mature.

Or did it?

I thought about it all day, but I couldn't figure it out. Was Cheyenne right? Was I really immature and just didn't know it?

Finally, I couldn't stand it any more. I had to know.

'Do you guys think I'm immature?' I asked Caroline, Sophie, Erica and Rosemary as we were walking home from school that day. Normally Rosemary took the bus to and from school, but her mom was going to swing by to pick her up from my house later so she could make another Mewsie film, since the last one didn't turn out as well as she wanted.

'No,' Caroline said. 'Who told you you were immature?'

'Cheyenne,' I said.

'Who cares what *she* thinks?' Rosemary asked scornfully.

Sophie sucked in her breath. 'She told me I was immature too!'

'She did?' I was shocked to hear this. I think Sophie is actually quite mature. She has four purses, including an imitation Dolce & Gabbana one her mother bought her in Chinatown in New York City. 'When?'

'The other day when she told me I should just go up to Prince Peter and tell him my true feelings for him,' Sophie said. 'She said if I did this, then Prince Peter would ask me to go with him.'

Rosemary made a gagging noise.

'Go where?' Erica asked curiously.

'That's what I said!' Sophie cried. 'That's when Cheyenne laughed and told me I was immature.'

Caroline pressed her lips together until her mouth was a flat line. She only does this when she's very, very angry.

'She doesn't have any right,' she said. 'She can't tell us what to do!'

'She's telling everyone else what to do,' I said. 'She's got every girl in the class playing her stupid Kissing Game.'

'Except us,' Rosemary pointed out.

'Except us,' I corrected myself.

'I heard Cheyenne is having a spa slumber party this weekend,' Sophie said.

'What's that?' Erica wanted to know.

'Everyone is going to the mall to get manicures and pedicures,' Sophie explained. 'And then they're going back to Cheyenne's house to do each other's hair and make-up, make bath bombs, sip herbal teas and watch makeover movies.'

'Why didn't we get invited?' Erica wanted to know.

'Who cares?' Rosemary yelled. 'Why would you even want to go? That sounds horrible! Herbal tea? Blech!'

'What's a bath bomb?' Caroline wondered.

'Still,' Erica said. 'I don't think it's very nice of her to invite every other girl in the class, and not us. Is that even allowed?'

'If it's a bomb you can use to blow up bathtubs,' Rosemary said, 'I want one.'

'Maybe Cheyenne just forgot to invite us,' Erica said. 'Or maybe our invitations are still in the mail.'

'I don't think we're going to be invited, Erica,' Caroline said. We'd reached my house, and were going in through the utility-room door. 'I think we're going to have to face the fact that we're too immature for Cheyenne and her crowd.'

'Good,' Rosemary declared. 'I'm glad they think I'm immature if it means I don't have to sit around getting nail polish put on me, sipping boring tea and making bombs for bathtubs.'

'Whoa.' Uncle Jay, who'd been wandering down the hall with a blanket about his shoulders (something he could be found doing most afternoons around our house, now that Harmony wasn't his girlfriend any more), stood there staring at us. 'Who's going to bomb a bathtub?'

'No one,' I said to him. 'At least, I don't think so. What's a bath bomb?'

'It's a thing,' Uncle Jay said, 'that when dropped into a hot bath it makes the water fizz and smell nice. I think it's supposed to make your skin soft. Harmony –' his eyes got a faraway look in them, like they always do when he mentions Harmony's name – 'sometimes used them.'

Caroline, Sophie, Erica, Rosemary and I all looked at each other with guilty expressions for reminding Uncle Jay of his lost love.

'What's this?' My dad's voice boomed out from the hallway, and I saw him coming towards us from the dining room, where he likes to do his paperwork when he's home. 'Girl Scout meeting?'

'Da-a-ad,' I said, embarrassed, as all my friends laughed at him, because he looked so silly with his glasses perched up on top of his head.

'We just came over to see Mewsie, Mr Finkle,' Rosemary said.

'Oh,' Dad said. 'Well, knock yourselves out. I think your mother left some snacks in the kitchen –'

A little while later after what Dad called a 'stampede', but I don't think that was fair, I think it was more like a dignified rush, for the peanut butter and crackers Mom left out – we gathered in my room so Rosemary could film Mewsie (since Mewsie is still a kitten and is only just getting to know his way around our ginormous house, he is only allowed out of my room when I'm home, and NEVER allowed outside, since it's winter and if he got lost he could freeze to death) and we could talk about Cheyenne's slumber party that none of us had been invited to (even though Erica kept saying our invitations were probably still in the mail, something only Erica believed).

'It's just because we won't play her stupid Kissing Game,' Sophie said as she ran the pink sparkle brush through Mewsie's long grey and black tail fur . . . except the tip, which is white. Also, although Mewsie likes to be brushed sometimes, other times he thinks you're playing with him and he tries to eat the brush, like he was doing now.

'You mean, you think if we acted like big idiots and ran around the playground screaming our heads off chasing the boys,' Caroline said, looking up from one of my Boxcar Children books, 'we'd be invited too?'

'Exactly,' Sophie said. 'Ow!' This last statement was directed at Mewsie.

'I don't know why you all even care about going to that girl's stupid slumber party,' Rosemary said. She'd gotten a good shot of Mewsie playfully biting Sophie's finger. 'It sounds like a giant snoozefest to me. Manicures and pedicures and doing each other's hair? Ugh! If you guys want to go to a slumber party so badly, why don't we just have our own?'

Caroline, Sophie and I all looked at each other. Even Erica looked up from the Webkinz she was arranging on my window seat.

'Hey,' I said, 'that's not a bad idea.'

Rule #7

If Someone Is Having a Party and Doesn't Invite You, Just Have Your Own Party and Don't Invite Them (and Make Your Party Better)

The Kissing Game didn't actually end up lasting all that long – just a day before Cheyenne's slumber party, Mrs Hunter and some other teachers realized what was happening, and put a stop to it.

Or maybe someone's mother called in and complained or something. I don't know.

All I know is, on Friday before morning recess Mrs Hunter slipped on to her stool where she normally reads to us (we were doing *A Swiftly Tilting Planet,* which sequels to *A Wrinkle in Time* and one of my favourites, besides the Boxcar Children, of course, although it's actually a completely different kind of story), and said, 'Class, I've been hearing that there's a new game some of you have been playing at recess – a kind of kissing game, where girls chase boys or boys chase girls until they catch and kiss them . . . I don't know the details, and frankly I don't want to know. What I do know is, it's going to stop now. I'm not going to say anything more about it. Except that if I see anyone playing it again, everyone involved is going to get their recess taken away for the rest of the week. Is that understood?'

Everyone in class got very quiet. Except for me and Rosemary. We both scooted out our chairs and leaned back so we could look past Stuart Maxwell at each other. Then we gave each other great big smiles.

To the vast majority of girls in Room 209, what Mrs Hunter had just said was very bad news. From where I sat, I could see that Marianne in particular looked as if she was about to cry with disappointment.

But to Rosemary, whose kickball games were always getting interrupted by hordes of screaming girls chasing down their prey, this was really, really good news.

And to me, who was always having to listen to Joey Fields go on about how come no girls would ever chase him, it was even better.

'High-five,' Rosemary whispered to me, holding up her hand behind Stuart Maxwell's back.

I high-fived her. I had to admit, I was feeling pretty good. If I'd known whose mom had maybe called in, I'd have given that kid a great big hug. Even if it had been Patrick Day's mom. Heck, even it had been Joey Fields's.

Joey looked like he could have used a hug too. He looked so upset, he was practically crying.

'I d-don't understand,' he whispered. 'Does this mean you guys aren't going to play that game any more?'

'*We* never played it,' I whispered back, pointing to me and Rosemary. 'Those guys did.' I pointed to Cheyenne, who had a pretty crabby look on her face. You could tell she was mad about Mrs Hunter making her stop playing her favourite recess game. What was she going to play now?

Oh, I forgot. Nothing. Cheyenne doesn't *play* at recess. She's too mature.

'But.' Joey seriously looked upset. He'd combed his hair that day and everything. 'Nobody's going to chase me now?'

I couldn't help rolling my eyes. Boys. Seriously.

'No, Joey,' I said. 'Nobody's going to chase you.'

'I'll chase you, Joey,' Rosemary volunteered helpfully. 'I'll chase you and knock you down and even rub some snow in your face, if you want.'

Joey blinked a few times. 'No,' he said. 'That's OK. Thanks.'

At recess, Cheyenne and all the other fourth-grade girls who'd been forbidden from participating in their favourite school activity gathered in a tight cluster by the swings. We couldn't tell what they were doing, but we guessed they were probably talking about what they were going to start doing at recess now that Cheyenne couldn't spread her disgusting germs everywhere.

Since it seemed obvious they might come up with an even worse activity, I suggested we send a spy over to listen in. The spy I recommended was Sophie, because she was the prettiest and also the best at acting like she fitted in.

'Aw,' Sophie said, fluttering her eyelashes, a skill she'd learned from Jill in *The Silver Chair* of The Chronicles of Narnia, 'thanks.'

'No spying,' Caroline said firmly. 'If we send a spy over, they'll figure out what we're doing, and then they'll think we care what they think, which we don't.'

'*I* care what they think,' Erica volunteered.

'Well, I don't,' Rosemary said. 'I'm going to go play kickball. Goodbye.' And she left to do just that.

'They probably think we're the ones who told on them,' I said, looking over at the group of girls by the swings. 'The reason I can tell is, they keep looking over here.'

One way you can tell that people are talking about you is if they look over at you a lot while they are talking to other people. This is a rule.

'Just ignore them,' Caroline said. 'Come on, let's go to our secret place.'

'It's not really a secret any more,' Sophie pointed out as we crossed the playground, resolutely not looking in the direction of Cheyenne and her friends, 'if everybody else knows about it.'

'You guys,' Erica said as we were walking.

'That's OK,' Caroline said. 'How are the organizational plans going for the slumber party tomorrow night, Allie?'

'Excellent,' I said. We had decided that the slumber party would be at my place, because I was the one who had gotten Dance Party America for Christmas. It was going to be a Dance Party America marathon slumber party. We were going to play it until our feet fell off. The reason we were going to get to do this was because my mom and dad were going to a faculty party at the university and were going to be out until after midnight, so Uncle Jay was going to be babysitting. And Uncle Jay was the best babysitter in the whole world!

'You guys,' Erica said again. 'Don't look now, but I think we're being followed.'

We all turned to look behind us. Erica was right. Cheyenne, leading a pack of girls that included Marianne, Dominique, Shamira, Rosie and even shy Elizabeth and some girls from Room 208, was tromping in the dirty snow right behind us.

None of them seemed too happy either.

'I said not to look,' Erica whispered.

We'd just been starting up the little slope that led to the bushes that hid the entrance to our secret hideout too. We couldn't exactly duck into it. Not with all those girls watching. They'd know exactly where it was.

'Hey,' Cheyenne said in a very mean voice, staring right at us. So it was very clear she meant us.

Still, Caroline looked all around and then pointed at herself and went, 'Who? Us?'

Caroline was stalling for time. I knew she was hoping if she kept on doing so, with luck the bell would ring soon. Caroline is very clever in this way.

'Yeah, you,' Cheyenne said. Today she was dressed, as usual, in the height of Canadian chic (which is a French word for stylish) in her knee-high zip-up boots, brown striped tights, a corduroy miniskirt, a puffy sky-blue parka and rabbit-fur earmuffs.

I wondered if she knew a rabbit had died to make those earmuffs. It is one thing to wear leather, which comes from cows, which we also eat.

But I don't know anyone who eats rabbits. Except French people, according to Erica's brother, John.

But John is a known liar.

'Which one of you told on us about the Kissing Game?' Cheyenne wanted to know. 'We know it was one of you. So you might as well just tell us.'

'Yeah,' Dominique and Marianne and some of the other girls yelled, 'just tell us!'

Erica and Caroline and Sophie and I just looked at each other. Because obviously none of *us* had told.

'Um,' Caroline said, looking down from the slope at Cheyenne and the other girls, 'we don't know what you're talking about. We actually have better things to do than concern ourselves with you and your stupid recess activities.'

'Yeah,' Sophie said. And so I said, '*Yeah*,' too, to back her up. Erica just looked scared.

'Don't lie,' Cheyenne said in a mean-sounding voice. 'None of us told. And you don't think any of the boys told, do you? They like it. So it *had* to be one of you.'

'Actually,' I said, 'the boys *don't* like it, Cheyenne. Why do you think they run from you?'

'Yeah,' Sophie said. 'Duh.'

'Don't be such a baby,' Cheyenne shot back. 'They run because it's part of the game. I'm kissing them. Of *course* they like it. They're boys, aren't they? All boys want girls to kiss them.'

'No they don't,' I said. 'They think it's gross. Especially your cranberry lipgloss. They think it stinks.'

Dominique, standing behind Cheyenne, started laughing when she heard this. Cheyenne turned around and stared at Dominique. So Dominique quit laughing. Then Cheyenne turned around and stared at me.

'Who told you that? About my lipgloss?' Cheyenne asked me.

'Stuart Maxwell told me,' I said.

'You're a liar,' Cheyenne said.

'No I'm not,' I said. 'Why would I lie about that? Stuart told me himself. I sit right next to him. Remember? If anybody told on you about your stupid game, it was probably Stuart's mom. Bet he told her what he told me, and she called Mrs Hunter.'

'*Yeah*,' Caroline said, narrowing her eyes at them. Sophie joined her by saying *Yeah* too, and Erica added her own, *Uh-huh!*

'Whatever,' Cheyenne said, waving her hand like our words were flies that were annoying her. 'I don't have time for big babies like you. That's why you're not invited to my slumber party. Because you're too immature.'

I put my mittened hands on my hips and yelled (even though Cheyenne had turned away and so had the other girls), 'Oh yeah? Well, you're not invited to my slumber party, either! And we're doing totally cool stuff, not boring stuff like you're doing at your slumber party, like getting our toenails painted!'

'Oh yeah?' Cheyenne looked over her shoulder at us, but not like she was actually interested in what I was saying. More like she was bored and getting ready to yawn. 'Like what?'

'Like playing Dance Party America,' I yelled at her. 'Until our feet fall off! That's what!'

'That silly game?' Cheyenne laughed. Her laugh was as bright and tinkly as the icicles hanging off the side of the school that Mr Elkhart, the custodial arts manager, had had to go up and try to break off with a broom handle so they wouldn't fall during recess and pierce some kid's skull and enter his brain and kill him instantly. 'We stopped playing that back in Canada years ago. Everyone knows the only cool game now is Captain Air Guitar. Do you even *have* Captain Air Guitar?'

I didn't know what she was talking about. I just

stared at her blankly. I had never even heard of Captain Air Guitar. Well, maybe I had. But I'd forgotten to ask Grandma for it.

'I didn't think so,' Cheyenne said with another tinkly laugh. All the other girls laughed their tinkly laughs too. Then they walked away. Still laughing.

'Allie Finkle's slumber party is going to be the worst slumber party,' I heard Cheyenne saying, '*ever*!'

'Don't worry, Allie,' Erica hurried over to say to me, laying a comforting hand on my shoulder. 'Your slumber party isn't going to be the worst ever. I bet it's going to be great.'

'Yeah,' Sophie said, sounding mad. 'She doesn't know what she's talking about. Whoever heard of Captain Air Guitar. That sounds like a stupid game! It must be from Canada.'

'Well, I've heard of it,' Erica admitted. 'My brother plays it over at his friend's house. But my mom says over her dead body will anyone ever bring it into our house. She says we have enough racket with John's new drum set.'

I knew what Erica meant. I could hear John practising his drums in my house, even though he kept his drums in their basement and his dad had put soundproofing on the walls. It was still loud.

'Who cares?' Caroline said, sounding mad. 'I'm

not interested in what the cool game in Canada is. I want to play the game *you* like, Allie. I want to play Dance Party America. I'm really looking forward to it.'

'Me too,' Sophie said. 'Except that Captain Air Guitar sounds like it might hurt my toe less.' When she saw the warning look Caroline gave her, she said, 'I mean, I can't wait for Allie's slumber party. It's going to be way better than Cheyenne's! You know what my mom told me? You can get infections from those manicure/pedicure places in the mall, because they don't always properly sterilize their tools, and if you have an ingrown nail or something and the germs get in there, you can develop a flesh-eating virus and if the antibiotics don't work your whole arm or leg might have to be amputated. I hope that happens to Cheyenne.'

'You guys,' I said sadly, realizing what they were trying to do. 'It's OK. You don't have to try to cheer me up. I know my slumber party isn't going to be as good as Cheyenne's.'

'*No, it is*,' Caroline, Erica and Sophie hastened to assure me.

But I knew the truth. Even though Mrs Hunter had put a stop to the Kissing Game, Cheyenne had won. Her slumber party was going to be cooler than mine and there was nothing I could do about it.

I felt depressed about it the whole rest of the day. When I got home from the school, I even joined Uncle Jay on the couch where he'd been lying pretty much non-stop all week, except when he got up to go to his classes, the bathroom and Wong Lee's Noodle Emporium, and of course Pizza Express to get a slice.

'Hey, chum,' Uncle Jay said, turning down the volume of the Top Twenty Video Countdown, which Mom had asked him especially not to watch when us kids were around. But Mom was still at work. 'Why so glum?'

'This girl at school said her slumber party was going to be better than my slumber party,' I said, heaving this big sigh. 'She thinks she's more mature than me just because she wears high-heeled zip-up boots and she likes to kiss boys at recess.'

'The slumber party you're having tomorrow night?' Uncle Jay asked. 'The slumber party I'm going to be in charge of because your mom and dad aren't going to be home?'

'Yeah,' I said.

'Do you really think I'm going to let you and your

friends have a bad time?' Uncle Jay wanted to know. 'Me? Uncle Jay? Have I ever let you down before?'

I just looked at him. Uncle Jay's goatee was now a full-on beard. There were crumbs in it.

'Um,' I said. The thing was, you can break up with boyfriends before they let you down. But you can't break up with people in your family. You can stop talking to them, I guess, like Mom was pretty much doing to Uncle Jay, and to Dad too, for letting Uncle Jay sleep on our couch (and in the guest room at night, even though he had a perfectly good apartment on campus).

But they'll still always be your family.

'I guess not,' I said to Uncle Jay in response to his question about whether or not he'd ever let me down before.

'Darn right,' he said, and held out his hand for me to slap. 'You're gonna have the best slumber party in the whole world.'

'OK,' I said. And slapped his hand with mine.

I didn't really believe him. But *It's impolite not to high-five someone back when they are high-fiving you.*

That's a rule.

Rule #8

The Worst Thing That Can Happen
Is for Your Secret Crush to Know Your Secret,
and for It Not to Be a Secret Any More

On Saturday night we started playing Dance Party America as soon as my parents left for their party.

About half an hour later, Uncle Jay came in with a batch of microwave brownie soup and five spoons, saying we should take a break. Microwave brownie soup is one of Uncle Jay's specialties. It's pretty much how the name goes — you make microwave brownies, but you don't cook them all the way, so they're like soup.

I was pretty sure they weren't having microwave brownie soup at Cheyenne's slumber party.

I was pretty sure they didn't do what Uncle Jay suggested we do a few minutes later, which was surf down the back staircase on Kevin's bed mattress.

It was OK though, because he made us go one at

a time and wear Mark's BMX bicycle helmet and my Rollerblade knee, elbow and wrist guards, for safety.

Plus we put the sofa cushions at the bottom of the stairs in case anybody fell off and had a hard landing. And Uncle Jay made everyone sit down on the mattress and hold on to the handles on the sides as he pulled it down the stairs as fast as he could, then jumped out of the way by the landing when it got going good and fast.

Of course with all the screaming (and barking. Marvin got a little overexcited) going on, Mark and Kevin came out of Mom and Dad's room, where they'd *promised* to stay and watch DVDs. It's horrible having younger brothers. I'm the only one of all my friends who is burdened in this way. Everyone else has older siblings who aren't at *all* interested in what they're doing. *Older siblings are better than younger ones because they have already been through everything that you are going through, and can Show You the Way* (this is a rule).

Erica swears this isn't true, that older siblings are worse, they try to boss you around, and also, teachers always say, 'Harrington? Was your brother/sister John/Missy Harrington?' and then look at you like, *Aha, I know what to expect from you*, even though you are nothing like your brother or sister.

Plus, as Caroline and Sophie and Rosemary say, with younger siblings, you can boss them around. Which *is* true . . .

But look at my slumber party! I had told Mark and Kevin not to come out of Mom and Dad's room, and even put in some nice family-orientated DVDs for them, and next thing I knew, there they were at the top of the stairs, whining about when was it going to be *their* turn to get pulled down on the mattress by Uncle Jay. Unfair!

But I have to admit in the end it was pretty fun, because Mark got really into staircase surfing and appointed himself safety conductor, checking to make sure everyone's padding was on good and tight. I mean, really, if it wasn't for him, Sophie might have broken another toe, or something even worse.

And when we got tired of mattress surfing (because everyone's stomach hurt from laughing so hard), it was Kevin's idea to go into Mom's closet and have a fashion show. We looked fantastic! Rosemary played fashion photographer and took pictures of us with the digital camera on her cellphone.

And Kevin helped us put everything back exactly where it had been so Mom would never know. He's a surprisingly good folder.

Then Uncle Jay had the best idea of all: strap

bicycle lights to baseball hats with electrical tape and then turn off all the lights and try to find each other in the dark.

This was the most awesome game! Especially in a house as huge and old as ours was. We had an excellent time sneaking up on each other and trying to scare one another (this was best accomplished by turning the bicycle lights off). Of course, Sophie was too scared to let go of me, but she was good at staying quiet when I needed her to, and we scared the snot out of Rosemary, who said she nearly wet her pants.

So it was worth it.

Then when Uncle Jay turned the lights back on, Caroline said she was hungry and for more than just brownie soup. That was when Erica found the cake mix in the pantry and suggested we bake a cake, and Uncle Jay said he'd order a pizza from Pizza Express if we'd make dessert.

So we made a chocolate layer cake (with icing from a can we also found in the pantry) that was pretty delicious, even if a lot of the mix did end up on the hood that goes over the stove. Then we decorated it with flower-shaped sprinkles we found in a box my mom had marked *Save for Easter* (but I was sure she wouldn't mind us using it, she could always buy more) and some pirate gold that Kevin brought down from his room (I just reminded everyone not to eat it).

It looked so good that instead of eating it right away, we saved it to show Mom and Dad for when they got home from the party (Uncle Jay made us clean up the kitchen first though, because he said it wouldn't be as good a surprise if we left a huge mess. He didn't notice the bits on the ceiling, thank goodness).

And Mom and Dad *were* surprised. It was hard to tell which surprised them more: that we'd made a cake: that we tied towels around our waists and acted like waiters and called them sir and madam and pulled out chairs for them like we worked in a restaurant; that Mark and Kevin were still up, or that Uncle Jay wasn't lying on the couch for a change.

But they took big bites of the cake slices we offered them and said they were delicious. Except we forgot to tell them not to eat the bits of pirate gold. They found out soon enough though!

They were right, the cake really *was* delicious. We each had huge slices after my parents were done with theirs, and then Caroline finished up what was left (because she can't resist anything sweet, to the point that sometimes she eats way too much of it and has to call her dad and go home to take antacid. But fortunately that didn't happen this time, because my brothers were there, and they ate so much there wasn't much left for the rest of us).

Then we laid around in my room with the lights off, trying to get Mewsie to go in his pink canopy cat bed, and I told ghost stories about the disembodied zombie hand until everyone fell asleep.

It was basically the best slumber party ever.

I really couldn't imagine that Cheyenne's could have gone any better. I mean, yeah, maybe everybody got to go home with their own homemade bath bomb.

But everyone got to go home from mine with their memories of microwave brownie soup, staircase surfing, a fashion shoot, bicycle-light hide-and-seek and cake on the ceiling.

I really don't think homemade bath bombs could stand up to that.

And I was right. When we got to the playground on Monday morning, we saw all the girls who'd been to Cheyenne's house on Saturday standing around in tight little clusters, gossiping about something.

'They're probably talking about what a terrible time they had,' Erica said as we walked past one of the groups of fourth-grade girls.

'Right,' Caroline said. '*They* didn't have that incredible cake we had at Allie's.'

This made me feel quite proud.

'You guys helped with the cake,' I told them modestly. Because this part was true.

'They're probably talking about the flesh-eating virus they all contracted at the manicure-pedicure place,' Sophie said. 'Gross!'

It *was* gross! At least until Rosemary ran past us chasing after her ball and gasped, 'You guys, guess what?'

'What?' I asked.

Rosemary picked up the ball and hurried over, panting a little.

'Good guess,' she said. 'I heard at Cheyenne's slumber party they did prank calls. Guess who they called?'

We all looked at each other.

'Mrs Hunter?' I guessed. That's who I was hoping, anyway. Also that Cheyenne got caught, and Mrs Hunter called the police, and the police came and arrested Cheyenne and she was forced to go back to Canada with her family, and she would never, ever come back to Pine Heights Elementary School again.

'No,' Rosemary said. 'Patrick Day. And Cheyenne

asked him if he would go with her, and he said yes. And now they're going together. For real.'

We all looked at each other again. Then Erica asked, 'What does going together mean?'

'I don't know,' Rosemary said with a shrug. 'I just thought I should tell you. I have to get back to the game. Bye.'

She ran back to the baseball diamond.

Caroline, Sophie, Erica and I stared at each other some more. Then we looked around the playground for Cheyenne. We saw her standing over by the swings with Dominique and Marianne and a few other girls. Cheyenne was talking in an animated way to them. She didn't seem any different though, now that she was going with a boy.

Next, we glanced around for Patrick. He was playing kickball with Rosemary and Prince Peter and the other boys, including my brother Mark.

Patrick didn't appear any different than he had on Friday, before he'd started 'going with' Cheyenne.

'This is weird,' Caroline said at last.

'What does it mean?' Sophie wondered.

'I don't think I've ever even heard of any fourth-graders who were going together,' Erica said. 'My brother is in the eighth grade, and he isn't even going with anyone.'

'Neither is my Uncle Jay,' I pointed out. 'And he's in college. But,' I added, 'he just broke up with someone.'

'That can't be the same thing,' Caroline said. 'I mean, your Uncle Jay and Harmony are grown-ups and kiss for real.'

'Why would Cheyenne even want to kiss Patrick?' I wondered aloud. 'Considering he picks his nose and eats it.'

All three of the other girls made noises like they were going to throw up, and Sophie said, 'Thanks, Allie! I had eggs for breakfast!'

'Well,' I said in my own defence, 'I sit in the same row as he does. Do you think I don't observe these things?'

'Maybe if you told Cheyenne,' Caroline suggested.

'No,' Erica cried, 'you can't! I'm sure he doesn't mean to!'

'How can you pick your own nose and eat it by *accident*?' Sophie wanted to know.

'Come on,' Erica said. 'He's not that bad.'

'Erica,' Caroline said, 'remember in second grade when he—'

'*Hello, girls.*'

We all stopped talking as we realized Cheyenne had strolled up behind us, Dominique and Marianne, her human shadows, on either side of her. She stood with her arms folded across her chest, staring at us, a little smile on her lips.

'So I hear you had a little sleepover of your own on Saturday night,' she said.

'Yeah,' I said, 'we did. And we had a really fun time. We did Dance Party America and staircase surfing, and made microwave brownie soup and a cake, and played bicycle-light hide-and-seek, and told ghost stories and—'

Cheyenne started laughing. Really. She threw back her bunny-ear-muffed head and laughed.

'You guys are such big babies!' she cried. 'That's the kind of stuff we did at sleepovers back in Grade Three. Right, M and D?'

M and D – which I guess were Marianne's and Dominique's new nicknames – both nodded and laughed. I didn't actually know them in the third grade – what people from Canada called Grade Three – but I was pretty sure they'd never had microwave brownie soup before. That's an invention only my Uncle Jay had come up with. So M and D were pretty much liars as far as I was concerned. As was Cheyenne.

'But anyway,' she said before I could accuse her of being what she was. A big liar. 'That's not what I came over to talk to you guys about. I came over to see if you'd heard the news.'

'If you mean the news about you and Patrick Day,' Caroline said, 'we've heard. And you have our condolences.'

Even though she claims to be so mature and all, I don't know if Cheyenne knew what condolences meant. She wasn't the second runner-up district spelling champ, like Caroline was.

'Thanks,' Cheyenne said. She obviously *didn't* know what condolences meant. 'He *really* likes me. It was just a matter of time before we started going together.'

'But that's what I don't understand,' Erica said. 'Where are you going?'

Cheyenne looked at Erica in a surprised sort of way. Then she started laughing. Behind her, Marianne and Dominique started laughing too.

'Oh, E,' Cheyenne said. 'You're so cute! You don't *go* anywhere when you're going with a boy. You're just going together. It's a figure of speech.'

'It is?' Erica threw the rest of us a puzzled look. I don't know about Sophie or Caroline, but I didn't understand it any better than Erica.

'Yes,' Cheyenne said. 'All it means is that Patrick

and I are an exclusive couple, and he can't go with anyone else while he's with me.'

Erica threw us another look, which very clearly stated, *Who* else *would Patrick go with?*

But again, none of us had an answer.

'That's what I wanted to talk to you all about,' Cheyenne said conversationally. 'Sophie, I know for a fact that you like Peter Jacobs. He really is cute. The truth of the matter is, if you don't snatch him up, some other girl is going to. So you better ask him to go with you soon, or you'll lose him.'

I whipped my head around to stare at Sophie. I was just in time to see all the blood drain from her face. It was pretty cold out, so seeing her go from having such rosy cheeks to suddenly being white as paper was really quite dramatic.

'But,' Sophie said, her voice sounding faint, 'I don't want to go with Peter.'

'Don't be ridiculous,' Cheyenne said. 'Of course you do. Just go up to him and ask him. That's what I did with Patrick. Well, I did it over the phone. But it's the same thing, really.'

'I . . . I . . .' Sophie looked as if someone had just told her she'd contracted a flesh-eating virus. 'I don't *want* to.'

'That doesn't matter,' Cheyenne said. 'You *have* to.'

'She doesn't *have* to do anything,' Caroline said, taking a step forward. 'You can't tell her what to do.'

'Uh,' Cheyenne said, flicking a bored glance over at Caroline, 'yes, I can, actually. Because if she doesn't ask Peter to go with her, I'll tell him that Sophie likes him.'

Sophie gasped.

It was the gasp of a girl who had just found out there were even worse things than flesh-eating viruses.

Even Caroline looked confused.

'I don't understand,' she said. 'So what if Cheyenne tells him you like him? If you ask him to go with you, he'll know you like him—'

'No, he won't,' Cheyenne said, looking scornful. 'He'll just know you want to *go* with him. But if you don't ask him and I tell him you *like* him, then he'll know for sure.'

This was so confusing, it was giving me a little bit of a headache, like when I ate ice cream down at the Dairy Queen too fast.

'Why would you do that?' Caroline demanded. 'Why would you do something so mean?'

Cheyenne looked genuinely puzzled.

'Because I'm trying to help. Help you guys not be so immature.' To Sophie she said, 'You have until morning recess to decide what you want to do. Come, M and D.'

Then she and her posse took off, Cheyenne's high-heeled boots crunching in the snow.

'Well, I don't care what she says,' Caroline said when they were gone. 'You're not going to do it, are you, Sophie?'

But when we looked at Sophie, we all knew.

She *was* going to do it.

'Of course I am,' she said miserably. 'I have to. Because the worst thing that can happen is for your secret crush to know your secret, and for it not to be a secret any more.'

'What?' Caroline looked stunned. 'That's not true. That's not the worst thing that can happen at all. The worst thing that can happen is that your parents could be killed in a car crash. Or that you get that thing you keep talking about . . . that flesh-eating virus. Who cares if Prince Peter knows if you like him? I mean, you do. So. So what?'

'Oh!' Sophie said, sucking in her breath like she was about to cry. That's because she was. 'You *would* say that, Caroline Wu! Because it doesn't affect you, does it? This is all your fault anyway! You're the one who told Cheyenne about Prince Peter in the first place!'

Caroline shook her head, looking as upset as Sophie. 'What? *My* fault? But . . . I didn't mean—'

'Shut up!' Sophie shouted just as the bell rang. 'Just shut up!'

Then she ran off crying.

That's really when it all became clear to me. That everything had changed. Not just in Mrs Hunter's fourth-grade class, but among the four of us queens as well.

And all because of a single sleepover.

Rule #9

Sometimes It's Better Just to Say Things
Will Be OK
(Even If You Know This Isn't True)

Sophie asked Peter Jacobs to go with her during morning recess.

And he said yes.

But this didn't cheer her up, like you might have thought. We found her sitting on one of the swings, very depressed. Almost as depressed as Joey Fields had looked, pretending to read his Boxcar Children books, back in the simple days of the Kissing Game, when none of the girls would chase him.

'But,' Erica said, confused. Caroline wasn't with us. Caroline had decided to give Sophie some 'breathing room' to 'cool off', and was playing kick-ball with Rosemary and the boys, 'I don't understand. If he said yes, why do you still look so sad?'

'Don't you get it?' Sophie seemed like she was about to cry. 'He only said yes to be polite. He didn't want to upset me by saying no. He didn't want to be rude.'

'Oh, no,' Erica said, sending me a desperate glance over the top of Sophie's woolly hatted head, 'I'm sure that's not true. I'm sure Prince Peter wouldn't do something like that.'

Sophie shot Erica a dirty look from her perch on the swing. 'Of course he would,' she said. 'He's a prince.'

'He's not a *real* prince,' I thought it was important to remind her.

But it turned out this was the wrong thing to say, since Sophie responded to it by bursting into tears.

'Oh dear,' Erica said, taking my arm and walking me a few feet away so we could talk without Sophie overhearing us. Not that there was any danger of this happening, since she was sobbing so loudly. 'What are we going to do? This is awful. Sophie is miserable, and I don't think, the way things are going, she's ever going to forgive Caroline!'

'I know,' I said. I was sort of wishing I was Rosemary. Because if I was, I'd have just walked up to Cheyenne and punched her in the face.

But I wasn't Rosemary. I was just me, Allie. And I'm not the type of girl who walks up to people and punches them in the face. I'm more of a non-violent-conflict-resolution kind of girl.

By lunchtime, Caroline and Sophie were in a full on fight. It started out as Caroline was apologizing (again) for telling Cheyenne about Prince Peter as we were picking up Kevin from the kindergarten class-room on our way home for lunch.

But Sophie wouldn't say anything back to Caro-line. She just took Kevin's mittened hand, looked straight ahead and started walking.

'Did you hear me, Sophie?' Caroline said. 'I said I'm really, really, really, really sorry.'

Sophie didn't say anything. At least, not to Caro-line.

Kevin, not understanding what was going on, went, 'Sophie? Did you hear what Caroline said? She said she was really, really, really, really sorry.'

'I heard her,' Sophie said to Kevin. 'My, isn't it cold out today?'

Kevin looked at me. We had to walk pretty slowly down the sidewalk because Mom had put Kevin in his snowsuit again, and he was waddling. 'Is every-thing OK?' he wanted to know.

'Everything is fine,' Erica told Kevin in a nervous voice. 'Isn't everything fine, girls?'

But of course everything wasn't fine. Everything was falling apart.

'Sophie,' Caroline said. You could tell she was getting mad now. Caroline doesn't get mad very often, but when she does, watch out. 'I don't know what you expect me to do. I said I was sorry.'

Sophie just kept walking like she hadn't heard anything. Erica and I, behind them, glanced at each other. Erica looked like she was going to throw up, she was so upset about the whole thing. Erica hates fights.

'I mean, I admit I should never have said anything to Cheyenne about Peter –' Caroline said.

Kevin gasped. 'Caroline told Cheyenne about Prince Peter?'

'Kevin,' I said, 'stay out of it.'

'But—' Kevin said.

'Stay out of it,' I warned him.

'See,' Sophie said. By then we'd reached the stop sign where Caroline and Sophie turn to go to *their* houses, 'even *Kevin* knows that was a stupid thing to do! And he's four!'

'Five,' Kevin corrected her.

'Whatever,' Sophie said. She'd started to cry again. 'You just don't know. You don't realize what you've done!'

'Oh, for heaven's sake,' Caroline said, rolling her eyes. 'Do you have to be such a drama queen all the time, Sophie?'

Sophie sucked in her breath again. Then she let out a wail, turned around and ran down the street to her own house.

Caroline, realizing what she'd said, cried, 'Sophie!' Then she ran off after her.

But ever since Sophie's broken toe has gotten a bit less tender, she's been walking and running without her limp. So I doubted Caroline would catch her.

Left alone at the stop sign, Erica and I looked at one another. Kevin was the one who said, 'If you ask me, they're *both* acting like drama queens.'

'Shut up, Kevin,' I said, taking his hand.

'Well,' he said, 'it's true.'

Lunch wasn't much fun that day. I had grilled cheese at Erica's house. We tried to figure out what to do about Caroline and Sophie, but couldn't come up with any solutions that made sense. When it came time to walk back to school, though we waited at the stop sign for both of them, neither showed up. We didn't know if they'd taken a different route to school to avoid us (or one another), or just hadn't felt like coming back to school at all.

When we got back to the playground, we looked around, but didn't see them anywhere.

'This is awful,' Erica said, slumping on to the root of a huge tree where we sometimes liked to sit when we came to the school after hours, just us two. 'What are we going to do? We're supposed to be best friends, but it seems like we're all just falling apart.'

'It'll be OK,' I said.

But I was lying. I didn't really think it was going to be OK. *Sometimes it's better just to say things will be OK (even if you know this isn't true).* That's a rule.

'What if Caroline and Sophie never go back to speaking again?' Erica asked worriedly.

'They will,' I said. 'They have to. They sit next to each other. Mrs Hunter will notice and make them.'

'She might move them,' Erica said. 'The way she did you.'

'She'd never do that,' I said. 'They never get in trouble for chit-chatting, the way we used to.'

Erica sighed. Out on the playground we saw Cheyenne and the other girls in our class, who seemed to have nothing better to do but follow Cheyenne around. They were all clustered around someone. I couldn't see who that person was, though.

'I can't believe just the other night we were all having such a fun time at your slumber party,' Erica said.

'I know,' I said. The memory pained me, like a kick to the chest.

Then the bell rang, and Erica and I both stood up . . . then froze when the cluster of girls we'd been watching broke apart and we realized the person they'd all been gathered around turned out to be *Caroline*!

'What's she doing with *them*?' Erica asked in horror.

'How would I know?' I was just as shocked as Erica.

We didn't have to wait long to find out what was going on. Caroline walked slowly over to join us, her head hanging low.

'Have you seen Sophie?' Caroline asked when she caught up with us.

'N-no,' I stammered. 'Didn't you walk back to school with her?'

'No,' Caroline said. 'I took the long way and went around the block. I was . . . I thought maybe she needed some more time alone.'

'What were you doing with those girls?' Erica couldn't wait any longer to ask. 'And Cheyenne?'

'It's a long story,' Caroline said with a sigh. 'And I want to tell Sophie first.'

Except Caroline wasn't the one who got to tell Sophie her story. Cheyenne got to do that too, as we were all taking our coats off and hanging them up back in Room 209.

'Did you hear the news?' Cheyenne asked Sophie, who'd gotten back to school late from lunch – probably on purpose to avoid having to walk with us . . . or at least with Caroline, not knowing that Caroline had taken a different route back to school in order to avoid having to walk with *her*.

'What news?' Sophie asked suspiciously.

I didn't blame Sophie for being suspicious. I'd be suspicious too. Every time Cheyenne talked to any of us, something bad seemed to happen directly afterwards.

'The news about Caroline, silly,' Cheyenne said. 'You and I aren't the only ones who are going with boys in this class. Caroline is going with someone too.'

I don't think my head could've turned fast enough to look at Caroline. In fact I think I almost got whiplash, which is a type of neck injury, from turning my head to look at her, I turned it so fast.

Caroline's face turned pink. But otherwise it didn't change expression.

'That's right,' Caroline said calmly. 'Lenny Hsu and I are going together.'

My head whipped around in the other direction so I could look at Lenny Hsu. He was the other champion speller of our class. Basically, he was second runner-up to Caroline. If you wanted to think of a boy to go with, you would never think of Lenny Hsu. That's because Lenny Hsu never talks or does anything at all except read books about space and dinosaurs. Which was what he was doing just then, not even realizing half the class was staring at him. In fact it almost seemed like if he and Caroline were going together, he didn't know anything about it.

If Caroline's sacrifice – because that's what it was. Caroline had no more interest in going with a boy than any of the rest of us did – was supposed to make Sophie want to be friends with her again, it didn't work. Because all Sophie did when she heard that Caroline was going with Lenny was turn around and walk to her seat with her nose in the air, looking about as prissy as she could.

And Sophie was pretty good at looking prissy, another thing she'd learned from Jill in *The Silver Chair*.

When Caroline saw this, she didn't start crying or anything. Her mouth just got all small, the way it always did when she was mad. Who knows what she would have done, if Mrs Hunter hadn't gone up to the front of the room and told us all to get out our English books?

I was pretty sure things couldn't get much worse after that. Much worse than two of my best friends being in such a bad fight that they weren't even speaking to each other. Oh, and both of them going with boys. One of them with a boy she didn't even like.

But I was wrong.

Because by Wednesday, almost every girl in Mrs Hunter's class was going with a boy except for me, Rosemary and Erica.

But even then, Cheyenne wasn't happy. Cheyenne was determined to make *every* boy and *every* girl in our class go together.

Because, Cheyenne said, that was how mature people acted.

So I guess it shouldn't have been such a shock to

me when I heard the news that Erica – my best friend Erica – was going with Stuart Maxwell.

Except for that part where hearing that news was like being stabbed in the heart with a knife. Erica didn't even like Stuart Maxwell! Erica was totally grossed out by Stuart Maxwell, because of his disgusting zombie drawings!

'Erica,' I said, the first chance I got as soon as I got Erica alone after I found out the news. We were in the girls' room, the only place Erica and I could talk any more without one of Cheyenne's spies finding us, it seemed, or Caroline or Sophie hanging around, talking bad about the other person. Caroline and Sophie still weren't speaking. Well, Sophie wasn't speaking to Caroline, and Caroline was so mad about it she had decided to stop speaking to Sophie in retaliation. Things had gotten so bad, the four or us hadn't played queens in nearly a week, and forget walking to and from school together. Everyone was taking a different route – except Erica and me.

But Erica hadn't said a word to me about *Stuart*. No doubt because she just wanted us all to get along and knew I'd be upset. But still!

'What is Stuart talking about, that you and he are going together?' I demanded.

Erica looked so miserable I couldn't even yell at

her, even though I wanted to. Erica and I have a tradition of yelling at each other when we're excited. But I wasn't excited about this. More like almost throwing up.

'I couldn't help it,' Erica said. 'Marianne passed me a note during math. She passed it from Dominique, who passed it from Cheyenne, who passed it from Stuart asking me. I had to say yes! I didn't want to hurt his feelings.'

I practically yelled. But only practically, 'Stuart doesn't have any feelings! He's *Stuart*! He likes to draw maggots crawling out of eye sockets. For *fun*!'

'He does too have feelings,' Erica said, giving me a reproachful look. 'Just because you think he's gross doesn't mean it wouldn't have made him feel bad if I said no.'

'Erica,' I said. I couldn't believe this. I wanted to throw something. But there was nothing in the girls' room to throw. Except toilet paper, 'you don't understand. Stuart didn't ask you to go with him because he likes you. No offence. But he only asked you because Cheyenne told him to. And all the boys in our class are absolutely so dumb, they'll do whatever Cheyenne says.'

Erica looked sad. 'How do you know he doesn't like me?'

I stared at her in disbelief. 'Do you *want* him to like you?'

'Well.' Erica looked uncomfortable. 'No. Not really. But I don't want him *not* to like me. I don't want *anyone* not to like me.'

'All Stuart likes is zombies,' I explained to her. I couldn't believe I had to spell it out to her like this. I couldn't believe one of my own best friends was so dumb about boys. On the other hand, Erica didn't have to sit next to boys all day, like I did. 'And making disgusting noises. Do you like zombies and making disgusting noises? No, Erica, you do not. You like gymnastics and cats and playing with your dollhouse. I'm sorry, but you and Stuart do not have a whole lot in common. I fail to see how the two of you make a perfect couple.'

Erica blinked at me tearfully. 'Cheyenne says if you don't say yes when a boy asks you to go with him, then you're immature.'

'So?' I couldn't believe what I was hearing. 'Who cares what Cheyenne thinks? She doesn't know everything.'

'But Caroline and Sophie—'

'Do they seem happy to you right now?' I asked.

'No,' Erica admitted. Then she sniffled. 'But there's

nothing I can do now, Allie. I can't stop going with him when he never even did anything mean to me.'

I thought it was pretty unlikely Stuart would even notice if Erica stopped going with him. When I'd left him, he'd been drawing a picture of a jet accident, in which most of the passengers had had their heads cut off, and their guts were spewing out of their necks, and birds were swooping down out of the sky to eat the guts.

He'd asked if I had a red marker I could loan him so he could colour in the blood.

But I knew Erica was too tender-hearted to believe that Stuart wasn't the type to be overly sensitive about a woman's love.

'This is all Cheyenne's fault,' I said as we made our way back to the art room. 'She has to be stopped. Do you hear me, Erica? She has to be stopped!'

'But how are you going to do that, Allie?' Erica asked, looking bewildered. 'Marianne and Dominique – all the other girls, really – do exactly what she says. She's got those boots . . . and she's from *Canada*.'

I knew Erica was right. I also knew it wasn't going to be easy. But somehow, someway, I knew I had to make everyone realize that what Cheyenne was doing was taking all the fun out of fourth grade.

Room 209 was turning from the best classroom I had ever been in into the worst one.

And I was going to change all that. Now.

I just had no idea how.

Rule #10

You're Only a Big Baby
If You Let Yourself Think You're a Big Baby

My opportunity to stand up to Cheyenne and prove to all the girls in the fourth grade that you didn't have to go with boys to have fun came sooner than I thought it would.

The very next day, at afternoon recess, Cheyenne came up to me while I was playing outfield in Rosemary's kickball game (now that we weren't playing queens any more, Erica and I had taken up kickball, even though the truth was, Erica wasn't all that good at it. Except the kicking part. She was more of a gymnastics kind of girl).

'Allie,' Cheyenne said, 'I need to talk to you.'

'So talk,' I said to Cheyenne. I noticed she had her usual gang behind her: M and D and also Shamira, Rosie, Elizabeth, and just about every other girl in the fourth grade except Caroline, Sophie, Erica and

120

Rosemary. Rosemary because she was playing first base, Erica because she was playing outfield right next to me, and Caroline and Sophie because they were at opposite sides of the playground, reading books and ignoring each other.

'Joey Fields is going to ask you to go with him,' Cheyenne said, getting right down to business. 'And you're going to say yes.'

Cheyenne pointed over at Joey, who was sitting on one of the swings, peering over at us. When he saw Cheyenne pointing at him, he straightened up and turned his head away, like he wanted to pretend he didn't know what we were talking about. Then he started swinging furiously. And barking.

I glared at Cheyenne.

'No,' I said to her.

Behind Cheyenne, a lot of girls gasped.

'*What did you say?*' Cheyenne narrowed her eyes at me.

'I said no.' I put my mittened hands on my hips. 'I am not going to go with Joey Fields. Now get out of my way.'

There were some more gasps.

But Cheyenne took the news pretty calmly. You could tell she'd sort of been expecting my reaction.

'Allie,' she said, 'you have to go with Joey. He's the

only boy left in the fourth grade who isn't going with anybody. And you're the only girl left. Well, except for Rosemary. But Joey doesn't want to go with Rosemary. Joey is afraid of Rosemary.'

'Well,' I said, folding my arms across my chest, 'that's too bad. Because I don't want to go with Joey.'

For a second Cheyenne looked as if she wasn't quite sure she'd heard me correctly. She cocked her head to the side the way Marvin, our family dog, does when Mark whistles really loud.

Then she said, as if she finally understood, 'But, Allie. You and Joey would make such a cute couple.'

I just stared at her.

'For real,' Cheyenne said. 'You both like those same books. Those what-do-you-call-them books.'

'Boxcar Children,' someone called from the crowd behind Cheyenne.

'Yeah,' Cheyenne said. 'Joey likes them. I see him reading them all the time. And I see you reading them too. So you guys have to be like made for each other. So go over there and tell him you'll go with him.'

I stared at her. 'Cheyenne,' I said, 'I sit next to Joey Fields all day long. Yeah, I like the same books as he does. But that does not mean I want to go with him. I don't *like* him. I don't like any boys.' I could hear my voice getting kind of high-pitched. Also, my knees were starting to shake like they had that day I'd first had to introduce myself to Mrs Hunter's fourth-grade class. A lot of the same faces that had stared at me that day were staring at me now.

But just like then, I knew I had to keep talking. I couldn't back down.

Because just like on that day, this was too important.

'I don't want to go with *any* boys,' I went on. I was practically yelling now. But I didn't care. I just wanted to make sure Cheyenne heard me. 'I don't *like* any boys that way. OK?'

I'm pretty sure Cheyenne heard me. I mean, she was standing right in front of me. Almost every girl in the entire fourth grade at Pine Heights Elementary was. I even saw Caroline and Sophie come from their opposite corners of the playground, having seen the crowd and I guess wondering what was going on. Most of the kids on the kickball field were looking over. Rosemary was annoyed at the interruption of the game, as were most of the boys. My own brother Mark yelled, 'Are we gonna play ball here or what?'

Cheyenne heard me, all right.

But that didn't mean she was listening.

'Only immature babies don't like boys,' she said to

me in a very patient voice like the one I've heard Kevin's kindergarten teacher use. 'Do you really want to be that much of a baby, Allie? I mean, you are in fourth grade now, after all. It's really time to grow up. I've put up with you and all your silly games – pretending you're a queen, and playing Dance Party America, and wearing those stupid snow boots instead of real zip-up boots like the rest of us. But the fact is, if you want to be accepted in the adult world, you're going to have to stop acting like a child sometime. Failure to do so could have extreme consequences. Are you ready to accept those consequences?'

What was she even *talking* about?

'Fine,' I said. 'I accept the consequences of not going with Joey. Whatever they are.'

'Fine,' Cheyenne said. She looked very, very disapproving and sounded more like Kevin's teacher than ever. 'The first consequence is that you have to go over and tell Joey that you won't go with him. And also *why* you won't go with him.'

I glanced over at Joey on his swing. The minute he saw me look in his direction, he turned his head away and pretended he wasn't paying any attention to what we were doing. When the truth is, it was so obvious he *was* paying attention.

Suddenly I understood what Erica had meant when she'd said she'd HAD to say yes to Stuart's note. If you're a nice person, you don't want to hurt another person's feelings on purpose. That would just be mean. It stinks to know you're going to hurt someone's feelings.

I didn't like Joey – not that way.

But I didn't want to make him feel bad (well, not *that* bad).

The sad thing was, I knew I was going to have to. And it was all Cheyenne's fault.

I rolled my eyes. 'Whatever.'

'Cover my position,' I said to Erica. She nodded, looking worried. Not about covering my position either.

And I started stomping over to where Joey was sitting.

The truth was, even though I'd said *Whatever* and rolled my eyes, I didn't feel like this was nothing. The whole time I was walking over to Joey, I felt a little sick to my stomach, remembering how sad he had been when none of the girls had wanted to chase him during the Kissing Game.

By the time I got to the swings where Joey was sitting, I was really, really wishing I could go back through time to that first day of the new semester and, instead of Caroline having big news about a new student starting at Pine Heights, her big news could have been that she'd gotten a horse instead.

Because then I wouldn't have been in this terrible situation. *Horses are way better than boys who want to go with you.*

Which is a rule. I just decided.

'Hi, Allie,' Joey said as I plunked myself down on the swing next to his.

'Hi, Joey,' I said. I tried not to pay attention to the fact that almost every fourth-grade girl was standing clustered on the edge of the playground, watching us.

'Do you having something you want to tell me?' Joey asked.

I noticed that Joey had taken his woolly hat off, I guess so that I could see he'd combed his hair especially for the occasion of asking me to go with him. His ears were bright red on account of this. You should never take your hat off when the temperature is freezing or below. That's because you lose eighty per cent of your body heat through your head. Sophie told me this once.

'Yes,' I said. I figured I better just say it fast to get it over with. Like taking a plaster off. It hurts less if you do it fast. I took a deep breath. 'Joey,' I said, 'the truth is, I don't want to go with you.'

Joey had been smiling a little, I guess thinking that I was going to say I would go with him. I was, after all, the only girl in the whole fourth grade who wasn't going with anyone (besides Rosemary, who'd made her position on not wanting to go with anyone very public). I guess to a boy like Joey, who was a bit of a romantic person (you could tell by his reading of the Boxcar Children books), the idea of my not wanting to go with him (since I loved the Boxcar Children too) was completely inconceivable, which means he couldn't even dream of it.

So when I said I *didn't* want to go with him, it came as a complete shock to him. He stopped smiling. Also, he grabbed hold of the chains on either side of his swing and started pumping.

He wouldn't even look at me.

'It's not that I don't like you,' I said, remembering that I was going to have to sit next to him every day, and it was going to be kind of awkward if he hated my guts and all. 'It's just that I don't like you in that way. That . . . going-with-you way.'

The truth was, I didn't even know what I was talking about. I was just saying some stuff I remembered Caroline and Sophie and Erica and I had said when we'd dressed up in Missy's clothes and pretended to be teenagers. It was stuff I'd seen teenagers say on TV. It sounded good to me.

It must have sounded good to Joey, because he stopped swinging so hard and looked at me. There were tears going down his face, but I knew from experience that they were tears from swinging in the cold.

At least, I really hoped that's all they were.

Joey Fields couldn't possibly be crying because he was *in love* with me.

Because that would just be way too weird!

'What does that mean?' he wanted to know. Only he didn't ask it in a mean way. 'You don't like me in a going-with-me kind of way?'

'It just means,' I said, wondering myself what it meant, 'that I just want to be friends with you. I mean, we're in the fourth grade. No one in the fourth grade goes with anybody. At least in America. Come on. You read the Boxcar Children books. Do any of them go with anybody?'

'No,' Joey admitted.

'That's why I like those books,' I said. 'Sometimes I just want to go live in a boxcar, and not have to deal with all this other stuff. Even if it would mean my parents would have to be murdered, and I'd have to

128

worry about starving to death. At least things wouldn't be as . . . *complicated* as they are now.'

Joey had stopped swinging entirely. I couldn't help noticing that he hadn't once, in our entire conversation, barked. Or even growled.

'That's why I like those books too,' he said, staring at me. 'Because they're about a simpler time.'

'Well,' I said, 'then you should be nicer about sharing Mrs Hunter's copies with the whole class and not hoarding them all in your desk.'

'Is that why you won't go with me?' Joey asked, lowering his head. 'Because I do that?'

'No!' I yelled in frustration. 'That's not it at all! Didn't you hear a word I just said?'

Joey looked alarmed. 'OK, OK,' he said. 'You don't have to yell. Jeez.'

'Put the books back!' I yelled. 'Just take them out one at a time. They're for everyone, not just you!'

'I said OK!' Joey yelled back. 'Stop yelling! Ruff!'

'And stop barking. It's really weird.'

'I can't help it,' Joey said. 'I just do it sometimes.'

'I know,' I said. 'I sit right next to you. Remember?'

'I know,' Joey said. 'You're a lot nicer than Rosemary. She use to throw Lifesavers at me. They really hurt.'

'I will never do that,' I assured him. If I had any

delicious Lifesavers, I wouldn't waste them by throwing them at Joey. I'd eat them.

'Are you sure you don't want to go with me?' Joey asked. 'I'd make a good boyfriend.'

'I'm sure you would,' I said as nicely as I could. 'But I don't want to have a boyfriend right now. I just want to stay a kid. And you should too. None of the Boxcar Children went with anyone.'

'That's true,' Joey admitted.

Fortunately just then the bell rang, so I jumped off the swing and ran to get into line to go inside, cutting off all further conversation. Of course all the girls clustered around me, wanting to know what I'd said to Joey.

'I said I don't want to go with him, of course,' I said. Only not loudly, because I didn't want Joey to overhear and be embarrassed. I mean, if there's one thing I know from sitting in the back row with a bunch of boys – which I'm not so sure Cheyenne and all those girls who'd liked playing the Kissing Game so much knew – it's that boys are human.

Yes, I like to say boys don't have feelings. But of course that isn't true. They do.

It's just that boys get over their feelings faster than girls. They just feel them, and then they're done.

Whereas girls feel, and then think about their feelings, and then maybe they write about their feelings in their diaries, and then maybe they call their best friend and talk about their feelings, and then maybe they tell their kitten about their feelings, and then maybe they'll talk about their feelings to their Webkinz, and then their stuffed unicorn with the rainbow wings, and then maybe they'll act out their feelings in a little play in front their bathroom mirror with a pillow posing as their best friend, and then if that doesn't work they'll act out their feelings with their American Girl Dolls or maybe some glass animals or maybe their dollhouse figures and then maybe their Bratz dolls too, for good measure . . .

Maybe this was why, when we got into Room 209 and were taking our coats off, and Cheyenne said to me, in the snobbiest voice I'd ever heard, 'So. Did you tell him?' that I just lost it.

I mean it. I just couldn't take it any more.

I yelled, 'Yeah, Cheyenne! I said no! I said no to Joey! OK? I'm not going with him. I'm not going with anybody! *And you can't make me!*'

And Cheyenne looked at me with her eyes all mean and said in a low voice, 'Then you know you have to face the consequences, right? You know from now on no one is going to call you Allie any more, but Baby. Big Baby Finkle. That's your new name. Big Baby Finkle. I hope you like it.'

Marianne, who was standing right next to Cheyenne when she said this, overheard, and started to laugh. 'Big Baby,' she said. 'Big Baby Finkle! That's funny!'

I don't know what happened. Somehow, Cheyenne had just pushed me one step too far. I mean, Big Baby Finkle isn't even the worst thing anyone's ever called me. I've been called way worse names. At my old school people called me Stinkle Finkle, for example. I got called Allie Stinkle – which is way worse than Big Baby Finkle – for like weeks.

But somehow, today, Cheyenne just caused me to snap. I couldn't take it any more. I just couldn't. Maybe it was how sad Joey had looked when I said I wouldn't go with him. Maybe it was the fact that back there on the swings, he and I had shared a genuinely nice moment when we'd revealed we'd both like to go and live in a boxcar (although in a million years I will never, ever want to live in a boxcar with Joey Fields).

And somehow coming inside and having Cheyenne be so mean about it just made it all seem so . . . I don't know. Dumb. When it hadn't been dumb. It had been nice.

So I just exploded.

'CHEYENNE!'

Everyone in the room froze.

'CHEYENNE,' I yelled, 'YOU ARE NOT THE BOSS OF ME AND YOU CANNOT TELL ME WHAT TO DO, SO YOU HAD BETTER QUIT TRYING RIGHT NOW. DON'T YOU DARE CALL ME OR MY FRIENDS BIG BABIES EVER AGAIN, OR YOU ARE GOING TO GET IT! DO YOU UNDERSTAND?'

Cheyenne's face went bug-eyed with shock.

In fact, most of the faces in Room 209 went completely open-mouthed at the sound of my voice and the words I'd said.

But no face looked as shocked as the one I saw standing in the doorway to our classroom.

'*Allie Finkle!*' Mrs Hunter was staring at me with her green eyes crackling. I had never seen her look so stunned.

Or so disapproving.

Rule #11

Speak Softly to Your Neighbour, Please

Mrs Hunter didn't send me to the principal's office.

Probably if I had been anyone else, she would have.

But I had never done anything bad in her classroom before, ever (except chit-chat with Erica).

And I don't think she actually heard what I'd said, just the decibel (which means volume) at which I'd said it. Also she didn't see who I'd said it to.

All she ended up saying, when she realized the person who'd been screaming at the top of her lungs in her classroom was me, was, 'Speak softly to your neighbour, please.'

Then she went to her desk, looking kind of dazed.

So did Cheyenne.

So did everyone else.

I think maybe their ears were all ringing from me using my outside voice, which is really very loud.

But just because I didn't get sent to the principal's office didn't mean that I wasn't scared.

What was going to happen now that I'd yelled at Cheyenne like that? Was she going to think of some horrible, even worse punishment than calling me Big Baby Finkle?

I could tell she was thinking about it. When she'd recovered from her astonishment over how I'd yelled at her, I saw her whispering with Marianne and Dominique and Shamira.

Obviously she was whispering about how she was going to get back at me.

A part of me wanted to throw up about that. It's horrible to be hated, even by someone you don't like all that much.

But another part of me was more concerned about Mrs Hunter and what she must think of me. I'd been a joy to have around the classroom before. She'd told my grandma that!

But it was pretty apparent she was going to change her mind about that now. I mean, what if she decided I wasn't such a joy to have around after all? I could see that she still seemed confused, looking from me to the rest of the class, trying to figure out what had happened. She seemed to think I'd been yelling at one of the boys.

Only the boys and I were of course getting along fine. Joey had taken out all the Boxcar Children he'd been hiding in his desk – seven of them! – and put them back on the classroom bookshelf (which was good, because they were seven I hadn't read before, and now that I was going to be the class outcast, and be hated by my teacher, I'd have plenty of time to read).

I didn't mind so much about the rest of it, but I just couldn't stand the idea of Mrs Hunter thinking badly of me. I loved her so much . . . I didn't want her to think I hadn't spoken softly to my neighbour for no reason. I had a reason . . . a really good reason!

And that reason was Cheyenne O'Malley. And she *wasn't* Talent, Not Talk. She was *all* talk and almost no talent, as far as I could tell. Her shirt had been lying! She'd been wearing a lying shirt!

She should go to jail for wearing that shirt.

Mrs Hunter didn't speak to me again the whole day. Which I guess wasn't that unusual. I mean, it wasn't like there was any reason to. I never raised my hand, or volunteered to help move the chairs during music class, which I'll admit wasn't like me, because I like to be helpful.

But Mrs Hunter must not have noticed my lack of helpfulness, because she didn't say anything about it. Either that or she just hated me so much now for not speaking softly to my neighbour, she'd decided never to speak to me again.

I was so depressed about this that I didn't even care when, as I was getting my coat to go home, Cheyenne sneered, 'Way to overreact, Allie,' in her snottiest voice on her way out of the classroom.

I had no idea what she was talking about. I guess the whole thing where I'd told her she wasn't the boss of me. Well, that hadn't been overreacting. That had just been telling the truth. Something Cheyenne wouldn't know anything about.

'I don't think you were overreacting,' Rosemary assured me as she walked down the stairs with me. Erica was with me too, and so were Caroline and Sophie, who had temporarily put aside their fight to show solidarity for me and against Cheyenne just for the afternoon. 'I thought what you said to her was perfect. I would have clapped, but Mrs Hunter walked in just then.'

'I know,' I said miserably. 'Mrs Hunter, who hates me now.'

'Mrs Hunter could never hate you,' Erica cried.

'She loves you! She trusts you enough to let you sit in the back with all those bad boys.'

'That's true,' Rosemary agreed. 'That's really a place of honour. Not just anybody can sit back there. I should know.'

'She just put me back there because I have brothers like you, Rosemary,' I said, 'and I'm not afraid of boys.'

I didn't add that I'm afraid of girls. Well, not all of them, but a lot of them. And how I'd started keeping a book of rules, mostly just so I'd know how to get along with girls.

I hadn't told anybody at this school about my book of rules though. I'd learned a lesson from my old school about that.

'So? It's still an honour. Cheer up. See you tomorrow!' Rosemary ran off when we got to the bottom of the stairs, to go get in line for her bus.

Which made her lucky, in a way. Because our walk home wasn't the most cheerful. Erica tried to keep everyone's spirits up and make us all get along, as usual, but with Caroline and Sophie still not speaking, it wasn't very easy. And I was still too sad to make much of an effort. By the time Caroline and Sophie left us at the stop sign, no one had really said much beyond, 'Come on, Allie, it will be all right,' and, 'Cheyenne won't dare say anything to you tomorrow! You showed her!'

But I knew they were wrong. Cheyenne would have plenty to say to me tomorrow, after she'd spent half the night on the phone with 'M and D' and the rest of her posse. She would have new ammunition and she'd probably make me so mad all over again I'd do something else to make Mrs Hunter shocked at my behaviour. Maybe this time I really would get sent to the principal's office!

Maybe I'd even get kicked out of school! It was possible that instead of being a good influence on all those boys I was sitting in the back row with, they were being a bad influence on me! Maybe, by the end of this semester, I'd end up in reform school . . .

. . . or jail!

But when I mentioned this to Erica, she said, 'Oh no, Allie, I don't think that's possible. You're good. Way better than Cheyenne. Did you see that shirt she was wearing today? It said *Naughty But Nice*. You're not naughty at all.'

This didn't make me feel better though. We all knew Cheyenne's shirts lied.

Erica asked me over for an afternoon snack and a game of dollhouse. She even said I could play the girl dollhouse character, and make her get kidnapped and then rescue herself if I wanted. But I said I wasn't feeling up to it. I said I just wanted to go home and maybe read some Boxcar Children. So Erica said she understood and to call her if I needed to talk. I hugged her and said I would. I let myself in through the utility-room door . . .

. . . and was surprised to see Uncle Jay letting himself out just as I was coming in. He had his coat on and everything. And Uncle Jay didn't have any afternoon classes that day. It was the first time in days I'd seen him up when he didn't have to be.

'Where are *you* going?' I asked him.

'I've decided that if Harmony won't accept me the way I am,' Uncle Jay said, 'then I'm just going to have to make myself into the kind of man she wants. I'm going to interview for a job.'

That's when I noticed he'd shaved off his beard. Including his goatee.

'Uncle Jay,' I cried. I was almost as stunned by the change in Uncle Jay as I'd been by everything that had happened to me that afternoon. His face looked naked. 'Are you sure?'

Something about the fact that Uncle Jay was willing to go against his principles after all this time and change just because Harmony had asked him to made tears well up in my eyes. I know our two situations are completely different – he's a grown-up man and I'm a fourth-grader, and Harmony was his girlfriend and he loved her, whereas Cheyenne's just a girl in my class and I don't care what she says at all. Well, very much – but still. The fact that after all this time Uncle Jay had decided to do what Harmony wanted instead of staying the way he'd always been made me want to cry all of a sudden.

'Hey,' Uncle Jay must have seen the tears in my eyes, since he poked me in the shoulder, 'don't look like that. I'm still the same Jay. Getting a job is a small concession to make if it will make Harmony happy. Besides which, I do need the money. Somebody has to buy turtle food for Wang Ba. And this will hopefully give me some good source material for my writing. Also, by conceding to this one small point of Harmony's, there's a chance she'll take me back. So it's a win-win situation. Any other questions?'

I shook my head. I didn't trust myself to speak, because I was afraid I'd start crying.

'Good,' Uncle Jay said. 'Wish me luck.'

I didn't say anything, but I don't think he noticed. I just got out of the way so he could leave. Then I took off my coat and hat, pulled off my snow boots, went into the kitchen for my snack, ate it, went upstairs, picked up Mewsie, went into my closet, closed the door, sat down, put Mewsie in my lap and started to cry.

I'd probably cried for about ten minutes before there was a knock on my closet door and Kevin's voice went, 'Allie? Are you crying in there?'

'GO AWAY!' I yelled at him. Mewsie, who was curled up on my lap, purring, stopped purring when I yelled. But as soon as I stopped yelling, he started purring again.

Kevin went away.

A little while later, there was another knock on my closet door, and I heard Mark's voice go, 'Allie? Kevin says you're in your closet crying. Why are you in your closet crying?'

'None of your business!' I yelled. 'Get out of my room!'

Mark didn't leave though. I could hear him breathing through the door. Mark is the loudest breather in our family. Sophie says there's probably something wrong with his adenoids, which is part of your sinuses.

'Do you want me to get Dad?' he wanted to know. 'Mom's not home yet.'

'No!' I yelled. 'Just leave me alone!'

Of course Mark didn't do as I asked. He went and got Dad. If you have brothers, you know exactly how big a pain they are, and why you can't really tell them anything. Because they will do things like this.

'Allie?' Dad tapped on the closet door. 'Could you come out of the closet please?'

I don't know why everyone was bothering me. I was totally snug inside my closet. I had my sleeping bag and all my dirty laundry piled up in there. Yes, it was dark and, yes, I was crying.

But I had Mewsie, who was soft and warm and purring and sopping up my tears with his fur. Why was everyone making it their business what I was doing in there? Was I bothering anyone? No!

'I'm not coming out,' I said to Dad. 'Please just go away.'

This seemed to surprise Dad. I guess that's because I usually do what he says. *You're supposed to do what your parents say.* This is a rule. A BIG rule.

Parents are supposed to protect you from getting hurt. This is another rule. And usually they do this.

But parents can't protect you from the Cheyennes of the world. Because parents have no idea that there ARE Cheyennes in the world.

'Allie,' Dad said in a different voice, 'are you hurt? Is something the matter?'

'No, I'm not hurt,' I said. 'I just don't feel like

coming out of the closet. Why can't I just sit in the closet if I want to? It's *my* closet.'

Dad thought about that for a while from outside my closet door. Then he said, 'Well, of course you can sit in your closet if you want to. But you're crying. Your brothers are upset, because you don't usually sit in your closet and cry. So they asked me to see if there was something wrong. Would you like to tell me what's wrong?'

'No,' I said.

'And you're sure you're not hurt?' he asked again.

'Yes,' I said.

Dad thought about this for a little while too. Then he said, 'Well, all right then. If you change your mind and decide you want to talk, I'll be downstairs, making dinner.'

'OK,' I said.

I heard Dad tell Mark and Kevin to leave me alone, that I just needed some time to myself. Then Dad went away, his weight creaking on the stairs as he went down them.

After a while I heard a different kind of creaking on the stairs, and then I heard Uncle Jay's voice outside the closet door.

'Hey, Allie,' Uncle Jay said. 'I hear you're in the

closet. I'm home from my interview now. Want to come out and talk?'

'No,' I said.

'Oh,' Uncle Jay said. He sounded kind of surprised. 'Well. Do you want to talk through the door?'

'No,' I said.

'Oh,' Uncle Jay said. 'Do you not want to talk at all?'

'That's right,' I said. 'I don't want to talk at all.'

'Oh.'

I heard some whispering, and then I heard Kevin say, 'I told you!' and then I heard Mark say, 'Shut up!'

Then Uncle Jay said, to me, 'Well, Allie, if you change your mind, you'll know where to find me. On the couch downstairs. Your dad is making your favourite for dinner . . . tacos. With no salsa. We know how you hate anything red.'

I didn't say anything. Really, what was there to say?

Finally Uncle Jay went away.

After what seemed like a million years, I heard the front door open and close, and Mom yell, 'I'm home!' Then she said, 'Boy, that smells good. I forgot it's taco night!'

Then there was some talking. Then there was some more creaking on the stairs, and then, finally, I heard my bedroom door close, and someone tapped on my closet door.

'Allie?' my mom's voice asked softly.

For some reason the sound of my mom's voice made me start crying all over again. I couldn't help it. I was just so *sad*. Thank goodness I had Mewsie to hold on to.

'I – I'm in h-here,' I called to Mom from the closet, my voice all sobby. It was a good thing Cheyenne wasn't around, because she'd *really* think I was a big baby if she'd heard me crying like that.

The next thing I knew, Mom was opening up the closet door. She didn't even ask if it was OK. *Moms are like that.* That's pretty much a rule, and you don't even have to write it down to know it's true.

'Oh, *Allie*,' Mom said when she looked down and saw me.

'I'm not coming out,' I said, still crying. I was holding on to Mewsie so tight, his purring was kind of sounding a little choked, like purr – mmrrph – purr – mrrrack – purr . . .

'That's all right,' Mom said, tucking her skirt behind her. 'I'll come in with you.'

And to my surprise, she did exactly that.

Rule #12

Tacos Make Everything Better.
Well, Almost Everything

It was strange, sitting with my mom in my closet. It wasn't something we had ever done before. Sat in a closet together, I mean.

But it felt a lot better than sitting in the closet alone.

'So what's going on?' Mom wanted to know. 'Why are you sitting in your closet crying?'

'Because,' I said.

And the next thing I knew, the whole story had spilt out. Everything about Cheyenne, and her *Talent, Not Talk* shirt, and her boots, and Mrs Hunter moving my desk, and the Kissing Game, and the slumber parties, and Cheyenne going with Patrick, and Sophie going with Prince Peter, and Caroline going with Lenny Hsu (even though I was pretty sure Lenny still didn't know he was going with Caroline), and Erica going with Stuart, and Cheyenne trying to make me go with Joey, and Joey crying on the swings, and Cheyenne telling me my new name was Big Baby Finkle, and me telling Cheyenne she wasn't the boss of me, and Mrs Hunter looking so shocked and telling me to speak softly to my neighbour, and Uncle Jay shaving off his beard and changing for Harmony . . .

By the end, I was sobbing more than ever.

'And now,' I finished, hiccuping a little, 'M-Mrs Hunter h-hates m-me!'

'Oh, honey,' Mom said, putting her arms around me. 'Mrs Hunter doesn't hate you. I'm sure Mrs Hunter doesn't hate you.'

'She does,' I assured my mom. The thought of Mrs Hunter hating me made me feel as if my heart was breaking. 'Everyone hates me! They're all going to call me Big Baby Finkle! I can never go back to Pine Heights Elementary again!'

'Don't be silly,' Mom said as she rocked me a little in her arms, just like she used to when I was younger even than Kevin. 'Let me ask you something. When this Cheyenne girl talks about you girls going with these boys . . . what does that mean exactly?'

'I don't know,' I said, shrugging. 'None of us does. Cheyenne says it's just what mature people do.'

'I see,' Mom said.

Being held by Mom was making me not feel so bad. I'd stopped crying just because I was smelling the Mom-y smells of her. She smelled like her perfume and, well, just like Mom. She was soft – in a different way than Mewsie, who'd finally gotten tired of being cried on and run off to go find his catnip ball and go swat it around – and comfortable and just perfect. Even if it was kind of getting cramped with the two of us in my closet.

'Well, I don't want you to worry about it any more,' Mom said. 'Because I'm going to take care of it.'

I felt so nice, like nothing bad could happen to me, sitting there in the closet with Mom, smelling her nice Mom smells and feeling her nice Mom softness.

But I didn't understand what she was saying.

'What do you mean?' I asked. 'How are you going to take care of it? You can't take care of it. You don't even go to Pine Heights Elementary.'

'I know,' Mom said. 'But I still know how to take care of it.'

Panic seized me. And suddenly, I knew. I knew what she was going to do.

'Mom,' I cried, struggling to get out of her lap. 'No! You can't! You can't call Mrs Hunter!'

'Allie.' Mom tried to hold on to me. 'What's wrong with you? Why shouldn't I call Mrs Hunter? She told us when we first enrolled you that if we had any problems, we could call her any time. Well, I think this Cheyenne girl is a problem –'

I agreed with Mom that Cheyenne was a problem. But I didn't want to be a telltale! A stool pigeon!

Although the thought of Mrs Hunter handling the problem of Cheyenne calling me Big Baby Finkle the way she'd handled the Kissing Game problem was deeply comforting, in a way.

Still. Everyone would know! And it wouldn't be like how everyone had known Stuart's mom had maybe called about the Kissing Game. Because that had happened to *all* the boys. The Big Baby Finkle thing had only happened to one person . . . me! I was the only girl in the entire fourth grade who wasn't going with a boy. Well, except for Rosemary, but she didn't count. All the boys were afraid of Rosemary.

'Mom,' I protested, 'you can't. You just can't, OK? Everyone will know. You have to let me handle it myself. OK?'

'OK, Allie,' Mom said, after a second or two. 'OK. If that's what you really want.'

'That's what I really want,' I said. Even though it wasn't. Not even the slightest.

Mom let out a big sigh and said, 'Fine, then. I'm going to go downstairs now. I want you to go wash your face and hands and get ready for dinner. Dad made one of your favourites: tacos.'

'OK,' I said. I didn't want to go downstairs. I wanted to stay in my closet, on my mom's lap, for-ever.

But I knew I couldn't.

Mom gave me a kiss, and then got up – with a little trouble – and climbed out of my closet. On her way out of my room, she wrinkled her nose and said, 'And don't forget to scoop out Mewsie's litter box. In fact, I think you should probably move it to the kids' bath-room. I think he's old enough now for you to can start letting him out of your room during the day.'

'OK right,' I said again.

After I'd scooped out Mewsie's box, I washed my hands and looked at myself in the mirror. My face was all red and splotchy from crying. I looked exactly like what Cheyenne had accused me of being: A big baby. I guess because that's what I was. A big baby who let other people boss her around.

Except I hadn't. I hadn't played the Kissing Game and I wasn't going with Joey Fields.

And I hadn't let my mom call Mrs Hunter.

Who knew what kind of torture I was going to walk into when I went to school tomorrow? Still, whatever it was, I was going to handle it on my own. Like a mature person, not a baby.

I dried my hands and went downstairs for taco night.

In spite of my nervousness about tomorrow, I was starving. I ended up eating three tacos with everything on them (except salsa). Everyone was very impressed by my appetite.

After dinner, we three kids and Uncle Jay had a burping contest, and I won. Mom said I was disgusting, but that she was glad to see I was feeling better. She also asked Dad when they had had a fourth child, because someone seemed to have slipped one into the house without telling her.

Uncle Jay knew exactly what she was talking about . . . him. He said not to worry, that he'd be leaving soon.

'Because,' he said proudly, 'I got a job today.'

'No,' Mom said, looking astonished. 'You did not.'

'Yes,' Uncle Jay said, 'I did. You are now looking at the newest delivery person for Pizza Express.'

Mom stopped looking so astonished. 'Oh,' she said. 'You got a job *delivering pizzas*.'

'Funny,' Uncle Jay said. 'That's exactly the way Harmony said it. It may not be the most upwardly mobile job. But every journey starts with a single step. And I get all the free pizza I want. And I should meet a lot of interesting people. Anyway, Harmony's going to give me a second chance. We'll be taking things slowly. But it's a start.'

'Hallelujah,' Dad said. 'I can have my remote back.'

'And I can have my guest-room back,' Mom said.

'Does this mean I'm not going to get your futon couch?' Kevin asked.

Uncle Jay told Kevin that, sadly, he wouldn't be getting his futon couch – a fact which Kevin accepted eventually (he got me and Mark to help him move his bed back to where it had been. I have no idea how he'd scooted it around to make room for the couch).

That night I didn't sleep very well. I kept thinking about how Cheyenne's face had looked after I'd told her she wasn't the boss of me . . . like I was about to learn a lesson. The truth was . . . Cheyenne actually sort of *was* the boss off me. Because Cheyenne was the boss of the whole fourth grade. I don't know how it had happened – especially considering the fact that she was the new girl, and she wasn't very nice. But somehow Cheyenne had come along and everyone in Room 209 had let her turn into the boss of us all.

And in the morning I was going to have to pay for standing up to her.

The thought of it made my stomach hurt.

The next morning I met Erica at our door when she came by to pick me up for school, I didn't tell her about how I'd shut myself into my closet, crying, most of the evening, or that I'd told my mom everything that had been happening in our class. I didn't tell her that I'd been up half the night worrying, or that, more than anything, I was dreading going back to Room 209 to face Cheyenne and be called Big Baby Finkle all over again.

I could tell by Erica's face that I didn't have to tell her any of these things. She already knew. She gave me a big hug and said, 'Don't worry. It won't be that bad.'

But Erica was just being Erica. It was absolutely going to be that bad.

And we both knew it.

On the way to school, Erica tried to give me a pep talk anyway, saying how if Cheyenne called me Big Baby Finkle she was going to call Cheyenne a name she'd come up with, and that she'd talked to Caroline and Sophie on the phone the night before, and that they'd both agreed to call Cheyenne the name too.

I didn't ask what the name was. I was too busy thinking my own thoughts. Which were mostly thoughts about how much I wished Erica would stop talking about all this in front of Kevin, who was listening very interestedly.

Which was why, when we reached the stop sign, I hardly even noticed at first that Caroline and Sophie were both there. Just like they used to be, back in the old pre-fight days! They weren't as chatty as before. But they weren't trying to kill one another either, which was definitely a step in the right direction.

I don't know what Erica had said to them, but she had gotten them talking, at least.

Erica totally had some kind of future ahead of her as a diplomat or something. Her skills as a queen didn't lie just in lobbing evil warlords' heads off. I guess all that trying to keep people from fighting all the time actually had taught her a thing or two.

I for one really appreciated it.

For the first time, I felt a little tremor of hope about the day ahead of me. I mean, in between the thoughts about how I was about to die.

Still, even though Caroline and Sophie weren't at one another's throats for a change, the closer we got to school, the twistier my insides started to feel. It had rained in the night, and then the rain had frozen over, so everything was covered with a layer of ice, making the tree branches all pretty and sparkly.

But it had also made all the old dirty snow completely treacherous and slippery, so that we couldn't go on the baseball diamond (Mr Elkhart was out there with the salt machine).

So that meant everyone was just standing around with nothing to do.

And it also meant that Cheyenne was totally just waiting for me the minute I dropped Kevin off in the playground. I mean, she couldn't play the Kissing Game (because that had been outlawed) or watch the boys play kickball (because it was too slippery for them to play), and it wasn't like any of them would talk to her . . . not even her alleged boyfriend Patrick, since he was busy trying to kick the ice apart, lift up chunks of it and throw it at people. This is what boys at Pine Heights Elementary did on very icy mornings.

So of course all Cheyenne's attention was free to focus on me the minute I set foot on school property.

'Oh, look,' Cheyenne called, the second I let go of Kevin's hand at the jungle gym (which was covered in icicles. No kindergartener was allowed to climb on it). 'Big Baby Finkle dared to show her face in school today!'

I set my jaw, even though my stomach twisted harder than ever at the sight of her miniskirt, tights and high-heeled zip-up boots. I couldn't help noticing that Marianne, Dominique, Shamira, Rosie and even shy Elizabeth had all gotten their parents to go out and get them high-heeled zip-up boots just like Cheyenne's. They were all wearing them. Their heels made click-clack sounds on the ice as they came towards us.

Looking down at my thick snow boots, I felt exactly like what Cheyenne had accused me of being: a little bit immature.

But if I'd been wearing boots like they had on, I wouldn't have been able to get Kevin to school without slipping, I realized.

'Cheyenne,' Erica said as we came down the path towards her. 'Why don't you . . .'

Cheyenne raised her eyebrows at Erica. Erica rarely, if ever, said anything mean to anyone. She was too busy trying to make sure everyone got along.

But today Erica surprised me, Cheyenne and everyone else who was watching, by shouting, 'Cheyenne, why don't you just shut up . . . *Big Mouth*!'

'Yeah,' Sophie yelled. 'Big Mouth O'Malley!'

'BIG MOUTH O'MALLEY!' Caroline shouted.

Cheyenne looked startled to be called Big Mouth O'Malley. Especially when Rosemary, who was standing nearby, starting laughing.

'Big Mouth O'Malley,' Rosemary said. 'That's exactly what she is!'

Cheyenne's face started turning red.

'I am not a big mouth,' she said.

'Uh, excuse me,' Rosemary said. 'But, yeah, actually, you are.'

'If I'm a big baby, Cheyenne,' I said, feeling a burst of love for my friends, who were helping me stand up to this girl who had been making me miserable for so long, 'you're a big mouth.'

'You *are* a big baby,' Cheyenne said. Her face was turning redder by the second. 'But I'm not a big mouth!'

Wow. Why hadn't I noticed before that Cheyenne was good at calling other people names, but she wasn't so good at taking it when other people called *her* names? How genius of Erica to have figured this out!

'Big Mouth,' Erica sang. You could tell she was kind of enjoying herself. She had had plenty of practice at home, watching her older brother and sister tease each other (and, sometimes, her). She knew how it was done. 'Big Mouth O'Malley.'

'Big Mouth.' Caroline, Sophie, Rosemary and I linked arms and joined Erica. 'Big Mouth,' we sang. 'Big Mouth O'Malley!'

'Shut up!' Cheyenne's face was so red now, it looked like a tomato. Tears were glistening in her eyes. 'I hate you guys!'

Marianne and Dominique and the rest of the girls from our class didn't know what to do. At first they'd been giggling. Because calling someone a big mouth was pretty funny.

But then when Cheyenne started crying, they stopped giggling as much.

Still, I noticed no one came to Cheyenne's defence. No one said, 'Hey! She's not a big mouth!'

I guess because they knew it was true. Also because they probably knew that tomorrow it could be *them* Cheyenne was calling a big baby, or something even worse, for no other reason than that they hadn't done something she'd told them to.

Suddenly, from over near the flagpole, the sound of a whistle pierced the playground. We turned around, wondering what it could be. Normally Pine Heights uses a bell system.

That's when we saw Mrs Hunter standing there in her dark green winter coat with its imitation fur trim.

'Room Two Oh Nine,' she cupped her gloved

hands over her mouth to yell in our direction. 'Get in your lines now!'

We all stared at her. The first bell hadn't even rung yet. What was she talking about?

'*Right now!*' Mrs Hunter yelled. 'Patrick Day, you put down that ice this minute and get in line!'

Patrick Day dropped the two foot chunk of ice he'd managed to pry up from the sidewalk. It shattered into a million pieces – just as he'd intended it to, although he pretended he'd dropped it by accident.

'What's all *this* about?' Rosemary wondered as we picked our way across the iced-over playground to get into our lines.

'You don't think she heard us, do you?' Erica worried. 'And we're in trouble? I mean, Cheyenne started it.'

'She couldn't have,' Caroline said. 'Maybe she's worried about the ice. You saw what Patrick was doing.'

I had a sinking feeling I knew why Mrs Hunter's class – and *just* Mrs Hunter's class – was being called inside early. Had my mom gone ahead and done what I'd asked her *not* to?

I felt like I had swallowed a fork or something.

My mom had called Mrs Hunter. She had actually called my teacher. I knew it. I just *knew* it.

And Mrs Hunter was going to tell everyone!

But wait . . . Mrs Hunter wouldn't say anything. When Stuart's mom had called – and I was pretty sure she had – Mrs Hunter hadn't said so. She'd just said the Kissing Game had had to stop. She hadn't said, 'The Kissing Game has to stop because Stuart's mom called.'

Maybe it would be OK. Maybe I wasn't about to get killed by every girl in this class (except my friends). Maybe . . .

Oh, who was I kidding? I was dead meat.

We got into our twin lines that Mrs Hunter required us to get into in order to march into school every morning when the bell rang. Only no bell had rung. Mrs Hunter stood in front of us, looking more disapproving than I had ever seen her.

Everyone thought it was because of Patrick and the ice. Patrick's face was even redder than Cheyenne's had been. Mrs Hunter looked up and down our rows to make sure everyone was there.

Then she said, in her coldest voice, 'Follow me, please. When we get into the classroom, put your coats and hats away *silently* and take your seats.'

It was clear that Mrs Hunter's fourth-grade class

was in trouble. *Big* trouble. We followed Mrs Hunter inside the warm building, aware that all the other kids in school, back outside, were watching us *and* talking about us. The first bell hadn't even rung yet, and they were all outside, still playing, while we were being brought inside to . . .

What? Be punished?

We didn't know. But it was clear it wasn't going to be good.

We didn't dare speak. We just went upstairs to Room 209, took off our coats and hats and mittens and scarves and went to our desks the way Mrs Hunter had told us to. None of us said a word. Joey Fields tried to say something to me. I think it was *Arf*, but I gave him a warning look, and he quietened down. I don't know about anyone else, but I felt as if what I had had for breakfast – oatmeal – was sitting like a tiny bowling ball in my stomach.

Mrs Hunter, instead of going to her desk and looking over her lesson plan for the day, like she normally did first thing, got the stool she usually read to us from, brought it to the front of the room and sat down on it.

Then she just looked at us.

She didn't seem to like what she saw either. It was as if what she saw was a bunch of maggots crawling from a skull, like in one of Stuart Maxwell's drawings.

'Last night,' Mrs Hunter began when she was sure she had our complete and undivided attention, 'I got a very disturbing phone call from the parent of a fourth-grader.'

Oh no! She'd done it! My mom had done it! And after I'd asked her not to!

I wanted to bury my face in my hands. Only I couldn't, because then everyone would have known the parent who'd called was my own. Instead, I tried to sit as still as possible, with my face turned straight ahead and my expression as blank as possible, as if I found what Mrs Hunter was talking about very interesting.

But inside I was freaking out.

This was it. I was going to throw up my breakfast all over my desk.

After that, I was moving to Canada.

Because I was never going to be able to show my face at Pine Heights Elementary School ever again.

I was praying, *Please don't say my name, please don't say my name, please don't say my name. If you ever thought I was a joy to have around the classroom, Mrs Hunter, please remember that and don't say my name.*

'I was extremely shocked and horrified to learn,' Mrs Hunter went on, 'that there are children in my class who are "going with" one another.' She said it just like that too. Like it had quotation marks around it. She even made quotation marks with her fingers in the air as she said the words "going with". I knew what they were, because we were learning about quotation marks in English.

'I have no idea what "going with" means,' Mrs Hunter said, 'but I can tell you right now that I will not condone it in my classroom. Any of you who are "going with" with anyone else in Room Two Oh Nine or any other classroom here at Pine Heights Elementary are officially broken up as of this minute.'

It was so silent in Room 209 I almost thought I could hear Mark breathing down in the playground. No one moved. No one even seemed to inhale. Everyone seemed to be afraid even to look at anyone else. Joey didn't even growl. I'm almost positive Patrick didn't pick his nose.

'If I hear any more talk of boyfriends or girlfriends or "going with" or kissing or crushing or *anything* like that,' Mrs Hunter continued, 'I will personally send the person to see Mrs Jenkins down in the principal's office. Then I will call his or her parents. Have I made myself clear?'

The eyes of every student in Room 209 were wider than I had ever seen them. I looked down our row and saw Patrick Day gulp.

'You are *children*,' Mrs Hunter said, her green eyes crackling. 'Most of you aren't even ten years old yet. You have years before it's time to start worrying about crushes and "going with" each other. You are *not* going to start now, this year, in my classroom. For now, you are going to concentrate on being nine. *Put your hand down, Cheyenne.*'

To my total disbelief, Cheyenne had actually raised her hand. At Mrs Hunter's tone, however, she lowered it pretty quickly.

She didn't look too happy about it though. She ducked her head, muttering to herself.

'If any of your parents have a problem with what I've just said,' Mrs Hunter went on, 'they are welcome to call me, either here at school or at home. I'll be *happy* to discuss this with them. In fact, I'll be making a few phone calls tonight myself.'

Cheyenne's head shot up. Now she looked a little scared.

Marianne and Dominique, I couldn't help noticing, also exchanged glances.

'Now,' Mrs Hunter said, sounding more like her usual self. Her eyes weren't crackling any more, 'in the future, I want you to know that if any of you is having a problem with any of your fellow class-mates . . . if you feel as if you are being bullied, or picked on, or even feel like you just need to talk – you can always, always, always come to me. That's what I'm here for.'

Right after Mrs Hunter said that, the first bell rang, indicating that the new day was starting.

Which was kind of funny.

Because a new day really was starting for all the students in Room 209.

Just in a different way than usual.

Rule #13

Snow Boots May Not Look As Good As
High-heeled Zip-up Boots, But They
Will Never Let You Down

By morning recess most of the ice had melted, so we
were allowed to go outside – which was good,
because spending recess inside was always fun for a
while (Mrs Hunter lets us play with her old board
games. The Game of Life is especially hilarious), but
I've always noticed boys can get annoying if they're
cooped up inside for too long. Possibly this has to do
with not being allowed to throw things at each
other's heads.

Of course, when we got outside, all anybody could
talk about was Mrs Hunter's speech. It turns out Mrs
Danielson had given her class a similar speech, so all
the fourth-graders in the whole school were talking
about it. At least, the girls were. The boys just went
off to play kickball in the wet puddles left over from
the ice. Rosemary wouldn't go with them, no matter

how much they begged. She wanted to stick around and see what happened with Cheyenne.

'Did you see her face?' she asked me. 'I thought she was going to hurl!'

This was an accurate observation. Cheyenne hadn't just looked like she was going to hurl. She'd actually looked like she was going to cry. I'd noticed right after Mrs Hunter's speech that Cheyenne had reached inside her desk, pulled out her pencil box – the plain one, the one that just had flowers, nothing else on it – and had slowly scratched out the big heart she'd drawn on it, with the initials *CO* + *PD* = *True Luv 4ever* inside it.

This, Rosemary had observed, had made *her* feel like hurling.

Now, standing around on one of the playground paths at recess (it was too wet for her to go anywhere else in her high-heeled zip-up boots, which, by the way, were suede), I overheard Cheyenne saying loudly to anyone who would listen, 'It doesn't matter what Mrs Hunter says. A love like Patrick and I share can't be denied. We may be too young now, but when we're sixteen, and we have our driver's licences, we're going to meet at the Brooklyn Bridge in New York City at midnight on New Year's Eve, and no one is going to be able to stop us!'

All her friends looked very impressed. I knew Cheyenne was telling the truth, because Patrick had already gotten Stuart to draw a picture of the car he was going to use to drive to meet Cheyenne – a yellow Corvette ZR1 with a supercharged LS9 engine, he said.

Patrick didn't have the car yet, but he was going to start saving his money so he could buy it in time for his sixteenth birthday.

I had to say Patrick didn't seem at all upset about the fact that he and Cheyenne had had to stop going together. None of the boys seemed upset by Mrs Hunter's speech from that morning. In fact, Patrick was more excited about the car he was going to get than he was about seeing Cheyenne at midnight on New Year's Eve seven years from now. He seemed way more upset about the fact that Rosemary wasn't interested in playing kickball today than he was about him and Cheyenne having to break up.

But then, I didn't understand what Cheyenne had seen in Patrick in the first place, so who was I to judge?

Caroline, however, didn't seem impressed at all by Cheyenne's announcement about their plan. She'd apparently had enough of Cheyenne, and proved it by marching up to Cheyenne right there on the playground and saying, 'You aren't going to be able to drive all the way to New York City when you're sixteen, Cheyenne. You'll still have to have a licensed driver in the passenger seat when you're driving at that age, especially if you're driving at night. I don't know what the driving laws are where you come from, but here in America they're *different*. You and Patrick are going to have to wait until you're eighteen at *least*.'

Cheyenne looked from Caroline to me to Rosemary to Erica to Sophie. Her face contorted with anger. Really, like a cartoon character's. I don't think I'd ever seen a person that mad.

'*You!*' Cheyenne screamed. Screamed. Right in the middle of recess. She pointed a leather-gloved hand at Caroline. '*You're* the one who told! Didn't you? You're the one whose mom called Mrs Hunter! Don't try to deny it! I can tell!'

I froze. I couldn't believe it. Cheyenne was totally accusing Caroline – wrongly – of something I'd done! Poor, innocent Caroline.

I couldn't let this happen. I had to say something –

'Wrong,' Caroline yelled right back at Cheyenne. 'It wasn't my mom. It was my dad!'

What was happening? What was Caroline saying? Why was she lying like this?

All the girls standing behind Cheyenne gasped, looking shocked. But before any of them had a chance to say anything mean to Caroline, I did what a good friend should, and took a quick step forward, saying, 'No! Caroline, what are you talking about? *I'm* the one who—'

'No, *I* did,' Erica said quickly, stepping in front of me. '*I* told. And my mom called Mrs Hunter.'

'Oh my goodness,' Sophie said, thrusting her small round body in front of both Erica and Caroline. 'No, that's not right at all. *I* told. My mom asked why I was so unhappy, and I said it was because you and I were fighting, Caroline, and when I told her why, *she* called Mrs Hunter. Last night.'

The four of us stood there, blinking at one another. I felt such a huge wave of love for all of them – Erica, Caroline and Sophie – I couldn't believe it. I wanted to throw my arms around them and hug them all. Truly, they were the most fantastic friends who had ever lived.

'You guys,' I said to them, blinking back tears, 'you don't have to do this. You don't have to pretend that your parents called Mrs Hunter. It's OK. My mom did it. I'm willing to take the blame.'

Erica looked at me blankly.

'What are you talking about?' she wanted to know.

'My mom was on the phone with Mrs Hunter for half an hour last night. Our beef stroganoff got cold. Missy was mad. But Mom told her some things were more important than her dinner.'

Wait . . . what? Had their parents *really* called Mrs Hunter?

'My dad talked to her for fifteen minutes,' Caroline said. 'She said she'd already heard from a few parents when he called.'

'My mom must have called right before your dad, Caroline,' Sophie said with a laugh.

Rosemary, who hadn't said anything, shook her head when we glanced in her direction.

'Don't look at me,' she said. 'My mom didn't call anybody last night. Except Pizza Express. I think you're *all* crazy. In a good way, of course.'

There was a squeak from the group of girls behind Cheyenne. Cheyenne whipped around to stare at Elizabeth Pukowski, who'd raised her hand as if we were in class.

'My mom called too,' Elizabeth said shyly. 'I'm sorry, Cheyenne. Don't be mad. But my mom says I'm not allowed to go with boys until I'm fourteen. She was super angry when she heard I was going with Robert. She's taken away all my computer privileges.'

It was just then that Rosie Myers raised her hand

as if she too was speaking to a teacher and said, 'Um, Cheyenne? My dad says I'm not allowed to go with boys either. Not until I'm sixteen.'

A few seconds later, Shamira raised her hand and said, 'I can't go with boys or get my ears pierced or a MySpace space until I'm eighteen. My mom says we have rules in our house and not to forget it.'

A couple more girls began raising their hands and telling Cheyenne what their parents had forbidden them from doing. Apparently, a lot of girls at Pine Heights Elementary had rules in their houses too.

It was right after that that an amazing thing happened, right in front of our very eyes. Cheyenne got so angry that everyone was saying they weren't allowed to be as mature as she wanted them to be, that she turned around really fast to storm off to be by herself.

But I guess she turned around a little *too* fast.

Because suddenly one of her ankles went out from under her in her high-heeled zip-up boots, and she fell down in a big puddle left over from all the melting ice.

Cheyenne got soaking wet. So wet, in fact, that she had to call her mom to come pick her up.

I swear I didn't laugh at her though, as she stood there dripping ice water all over the place.

Because that wouldn't have been very mature.

And I swear I wasn't happy that Cheyenne missed a bunch of school that day, because she twisted her ankle when she fell, and had to go get it X-rayed.

Because that wouldn't have been very mature of me either.

Besides, *It's wrong to take delight in the pain of others*. That's a rule.

Of course, it would have been too much to hope that Cheyenne was so mad about everything that happened that she never came back to school and decided to move back to Canada. That would have been too good to be true.

Unfortunately, she was back in school by music class.

But she came back wearing one of those bootees on her foot like Sophie had to wear for her broken toe. Because it turned out she had a sprained ankle.

She got a lot of attention because of it, and because of her crutches. But only from Marianne and Dominique, who volunteered to carry her books and things for her.

I stopped wanting a pair of high-heeled zip-up boots like hers though, because I had learned a really good lesson from what had happened to Cheyenne, and saw that my mom had been right all along.

On the way home to lunch that day, Caroline said to Sophie as they were holding Kevin's hands and walking him, 'Did you really tell your mom that the reason you were so unhappy was because you were in a fight with me?'

Sophie looked up at Caroline, who is one of the tallest girls in our class, with tears in her eyes.

'Yes,' she said. 'I hated fighting with you.'

'Sophie,' Caroline said. 'I'm really, really, really sorry I told Cheyenne about Prince Peter.'

'I know,' Sophie said. 'He and I are broken up now. I guess. I mean, it's not like we've talked about it. Not that we ever talked. Which was fine with me, because now I can go back to having a secret crush on him. It's much better that way.'

'Well,' Caroline said looking as if she felt a little guilty about something, 'Lenny and I were never actually going together. I sort of made the whole thing up about asking him to go with me. I don't think he ever even knew we were going together.'

Kevin started to say something about this, but I shushed him.

'Oh,' Sophie said as Erica and I exchanged stunned looks.

'Do you forgive me?' Caroline wanted to know.

'I forgive you,' Sophie said.

And they dropped Kevin's hands to hug one another.

And just like that, the four of us were friends again and everything went back to normal.

Really. Almost everything.

I still have to sit in the last row with those boys.

But it's all right, because I have my best friends to support me.

And *All you need is friends.*

That's a rule.

Allie Finkle's Rules

- It's the thought that counts.
- The best part about the holidays is showing all the cool stuff you got for Christmas to your friends.
- As a big sister, it's your job to take care of your brothers and not punch them in the arm and make them drop their new bikes in the snow and get them all wet.
- It's OK to lie if the lie makes someone else feel better.
- Wearing the fact that you are talented on your T-shirt is always a smart rule.
- Friendly people don't tell other people that their games are babyish.
- You aren't supposed to hate people.
- Boys can seriously be so stupid sometimes. Also deeply thoughtless.
- Just because something is popular doesn't mean it's good.
- Lying doesn't solve anything. Usually.

- Sometimes you have to use your reasonable voice to get what you want. Especially with boys.
- If someone is having a party and doesn't invite you, just have your own party and don't invite them (and make your party better).
- One way you can tell that people are talking about you is if they look over at you a lot while they are talking to other people.
- It's impolite not to high-five someone back when they are high-fiving you.
- The worst thing that can happen is for your secret crush to know your secret, and for it not to be a secret any more.
- Older siblings are better than younger ones because they have already been through everything that you are going through, and can Show You the Way.
- Sometimes it's better just to say things will be OK (even if you know this isn't true).
- You're only a big baby if you let yourself think you're a big baby.
- Horses are *way* better than boys who want to go with you.
- Speak softly to your neighbour, please.
- You're supposed to do what your parents say.

BEST FRIENDS AND DRAMA QUEENS

- Parents are supposed to protect you from getting hurt.
- Moms are like that.
- Tacos make everything better. Well, almost everything.
- Snow boots may not look as good as high-heeled zip-up boots, but they will never let you down.
- It's wrong to take delight in the pain of others.
- All you need is friends.